To Win a Highlander's Heart

TO WIN A HIGHLANDER'S HEART

A GUARDIANS OF THE ISLES ROMANCE

GERRI RUSSELL

To Renee,
With all my best wishes —
Gerri
Russell

TULE
PUBLISHING

DEDICATION

To my one and only Highlander: Chuck
You are my love, my heart, and my partner for life.

PROLOGUE

Dunvegan Castle, Scotland
Wednesday, October 31st, 1742

A WILD WIND swirled across Loch Dunvegan and through the gardens and the woodlands beyond Dunvegan Castle, scattering the mist, leaves, and flower petals as it wound its way back to the Fairy Cave.

From inside the cave's depths a light flickered and a wisp of breath joined the wind, as Aria forced her way through the thinned veil between the human and the fairy world on All Hallows' Eve. A portal had opened at midnight close to Dunvegan Castle and Aria would do whatever it took to break free of the fairy realm as the human world loomed before her.

As she struggled, her thoughts turned to the past when her mother, Pearl, had come to the human realm years ago and had met the laird of the MacLeod clan. The two fell in love and had married and she eventually had a son. Even so, the fairy king had called his daughter home after a year and a day of that marriage. Pearl had done as requested even though her heart was broken, leaving her son behind. It wasn't until later that she discovered she was pregnant once again.

Pearl had returned to Dunvegan shortly after leaving, when her son's distressed cries had reached the fairy realm. Her child had been left alone in the nursery by his nurse-maid. Pearl had hurried back to comfort her young son, singing him a lullaby and wrapping him in a magical cloth that had since come to be known by the MacLeods as the Fairy Flag. The flag was infused with magic that would protect the MacLeods in a time of great need. But the silken cloth could only be used for protection three times before it would return to Fairyland.

Pearl had considered telling Iain Cair that she was preg-nant with yet another of his children, but before she'd had the opportunity, Oberon had pulled her back into the realm of fairies.

Eight months later, Aria was born. As half-human and half-fairy, she had tried to fit in with the other fairies. Instead of acceptance, even as Oberon's granddaughter, they'd called Aria a mixed-blood abomination and tormented her. Her mother had begged Oberon to return Aria to the human realm, but he refused, saying no member of his bloodline would ever again be allowed to walk among humans, even if she were half-human. His enemies would take advantage of anyone outside of Oberon's protection.

Regardless, Pearl had tried to return Aria to the Mac-Leods thirteen human winters ago. The then laird's wife,

Janet, had tried to help Pearl and Aria and brought them to see the laird, Norman MacLeod. The chieftain had been enraged at Pearl's request that he shelter her daughter in his clan, allowing her to grow up with his own human children. Janet pleaded with him to change his mind. After all, the fairies and the MacLeods were not strangers.

The laird had refused, and instead of allowing them to go back to Fairyland, he tried to imprison the two of them, claiming they deserved to live out their days in the darkness of his dungeon. Before his orders were implemented, Janet freed Aria and Pearl from the guards, allowing them to escape.

At that same time, the fairy king had learned they were missing from Fairyland and had used his magic to draw them both back to his realm, along with a human baby boy who was to be Aria's mate eventually.

Aria's dream of living amongst the humans, of being treated as kin, had died that day, and a need for revenge against the man who had spurned her had taken hold. She'd carefully planned and plotted over the past thirteen years, hiding herself from Oberon so that he wouldn't know she was gone from Fairyland this time, and figuring out how to breach the barrier between the fairy and human realms. Today was the day her chicanery would bear fruit, and soon she would make Norman MacLeod pay for ruining her life.

Using every bit of strength she possessed, Aria thrust herself forward until finally, her other-worldly legs stepped into the human realm. A smile touched her lips when she saw that her bow and quiver had been allowed through the barrier with her.

She would have her revenge against the MacLeod chieftain who had refused to take her into his family. The laird's children, her partial kin, did not know she existed so it would be easy for her to hide until she took measure of the situation at Dunvegan Castle. Aria took a tentative step forward. The coolness of the winter night caressed her cheeks and she breathed deeply of the sea air. She had thought she remembered the scent of the sea from her previous visit, but she had not. The air smelled both tangy and sweet, a subtle scent that had no equal in Fairyland.

Aria looked left then right as she reached the entrance to the Fairy Cave. Others who were not of Oberon's bloodline had emerged through this portal before her, and now she wondered where they had gone when they did. Did they hide amongst the MacLeod clan? Had they taken other forms in an effort to hide in plain sight?

Aria frowned. She had no intention of hiding. She had come here to hear from Norman MacLeod's own lips why he had prohibited her from remaining with her partial kin. Then once she had her answers, she would take her revenge on Norman "Wicked Man" MacLeod. Only when he experienced the kind of pain she had endured her whole life would she decide whether to stay in the human realm or return to Fairyland.

Moving down the path, Aria caught sight of Dunvegan Castle. The golden stones of the hulking fortress were illuminated by the moon and the stars above. The structure was fearsome and almost ugly when compared to the palace where she'd been raised. At the same time, it was also one of the most beautiful sights Aria had ever seen. Every stone of the castle had been set by generations of people with her own bloodline. While the MacLeods were recognised as fully human by others around them, there was a mix of fairy blood in every MacLeod since Iain Cair's son—her brother, William—had been born.

A deep-seated desire for connection rose in Aria but she tamped it down. Now was not the time for sentimentality. Such emotions would only get in the way of her goal. To accomplish her mission, she needed to find a place to hide and watch the MacLeods. Only then would she have the information she needed to exact her revenge.

CHAPTER ONE

Isle of Skye, Scotland
Tuesday, September 12th, 1741

I SOLDE NICOLSON WAS the best warrior at Scorrybreac Castle, whether anyone wanted to acknowledge that fact or not, despite her size, despite her sex. She looked across the mist-shrouded lists at the men who would challenge her this morning. As they did every morning, the castle's men—both young and old—stared at her with disgust while they waited for the master-at-arms to arrive.

"You're an abomination," her cousin, Watt, said as he walked past her and bumped her with his massive shoulder. "Why can't you be a normal female?"

Isolde straightened, not letting the man's words cut her as his sword never would. For the hundredth time she forgave him and all the others who called her names. They were lashing out because in a few moments she would once again prove what they all feared: that she was the better swordsman.

Most of the men simply ignored her, except Watt, Richard, and Murdo. They spent every morning trying to intimidate her. They'd been doing it for years. When she was younger, she had buckled under their verbal and physical abuse. But she knew something they did not. Their actions had helped to hone her skills to what they were today. She could best any one of them with a sword and with her bow.

Ever since she could first pick up a sword, and then a bow, it had been her dream to defend her home and her country as a warrior alongside the other warriors. Her father had indulged her, giving her a sword and allowing her to participate in mock battles with her older brother.

Isolde had been fortunate enough to be educated alongside her brother, John, by her non-traditional father and mother. When she showed not only skill, but also aptitude, her father had allowed her to train alongside the castle's men and encouraged her to use a sword and also a bow. "To defend yourself from attackers both far and near," he'd said with an affectionate smile.

Her ambitions had never wavered, but fate dealt them all a blow when her parents had died, their ship going down in a storm during a routine trading expedition to Flanders. After their deaths, her brother had become the leader of the Nicolson clan. His acceptance of her skills and her presence at Scorrybreac had worn thin over the past few years. If she didn't prove to her brother what a valuable asset she was in the next few months, she was certain he would find a way to be rid of her in the way many men solved problems with unwanted females: through marriage.

Alaric, the master-at-arms, entered the list just then, saving her from her grim thoughts. When she was battling, she felt in control of her life and her body. Though she was not as brawny as her cousin, Watt, she had honed her muscles and her movements with discipline, training, and hard work. Her lithe form gave her an advantage over the hulking warriors who now gathered around. She could move quickly to not only avoid their powerful blows, but also to position herself for better striking advantage.

"Pair off," Alaric called out. All around her the men paired up, avoiding eye contact with her until only she and Watt were left. He groaned his displeasure as he drew his sword. "Are you ready?" Impatience flashed in his eyes.

Isolde drew her sword. She offered her opponent a brief salute with her weapon as she tucked the length of her dress behind her. She'd barely finished the movement when Watt's lip curled up in an arrogant smile as he lifted his weapon high over his head and swung with the full force of his strength at her.

Isolde did nothing to counter the move except to step back, allowing her partner to swing at the air. He stumbled forward, then sideways with the force of his movements. He growled in outrage.

These men were always so impatient to begin. Watt would be better served to hesitate, to think about and anticipate his foe, but he never did. Instead, he rushed forward, cutting and slashing this time as he advanced.

Isolde parried his blade, then with a jab of her weapon, sent him to the ground.

He hit the dirt with a soft thud, quickly rolled to his feet, and lashed out again.

Watt fought well, but not well enough to best her. Isolde leapt sideways then sent her blade whistling between his neck and his shoulders, avoiding harming him, but taking several inches off his beard as her weapon sailed by.

Watt's eyes went wide. "Are you trying to kill me?" His tone was filled with both surprise and irritation. Then his hand moved to his beard and a dark frown came to his face.

Their blades clashed again and again, and as they did, a pulse entered Isolde's blood, filling her with a sense of rightness. This was what she was meant to do. This was who she was. A warrior for Scorrybreac.

Isolde allowed Watt one last pass then, permitting her new-found invigoration to fill her, she pursued him with an intensity that caused his face to pale. With a swipe of her sword and a twist, she knocked his sword from his hand. Then with a sweep of her foot, she knocked his legs out from under him until he lay at her feet, conquered.

Watt stared up at the blade against his chest with awe, which slipped to anger a heartbeat later. "I didn't sleep well last night," he grumbled as he got to his feet. He always had an excuse. She never argued with him. It would only make matters worse if she pointed out that warriors often had to go into battle with little or no sleep.

He glared at Isolde as he prepared to battle once more, but a sound in the distance stalled not only him but all the others as well. "The gates are opening," Watt said, lowering his weapon.

"We have visitors," Alaric called out. "You may go to greet them, then I want you back here for more training. Agreed?"

A chorus of ayes sounded as the men streamed towards the front courtyard. Instead of joining them, Isolde sheathed her sword and picked up her bow and quiver before entering the castle and climbing to the north tower. It was her favourite place to watch the comings to and goings from her home.

High above the commotion, Isolde drew in a breath of fresh air. From this vantage point, she could easily view Portree Harbour and the surrounding countryside. Her gaze swept along the approach to the castle, watching a small company of men as they crossed the drawbridge then headed for the keep. Her brother had obviously invited these men here. Who were they?

She studied each man as he came forward, until she recognised one man amongst them all. Ewen MacPhee was thick and squat, and his constant furrowed brow and piercing eyes made him look like the scoundrel she knew him to be. This was the third time he and his men had visited the castle this week. And with a sinking feeling at her core, Isolde suspected she knew why. Her brother was planning to marry her off to the one man she detested above all others.

Ewen had attended a dinner with the Nicolson clan two days ago where her brother had hinted at a match between the two of them. All through the meal she'd thwarted most of Ewen's clumsy advances. And when he'd caught her alone, he'd groped her with his meaty paws and had tried to kiss her until she'd kneed him in the bollocks.

Still angered by those events, Isolde reached for an arrow from her quiver and set it against the string of her bow, with one finger above the arrow and two below. She located Ewen after he'd dismounted and, pulling the string until it touched her lips and chin, she aimed not at the man's heart but at the narrow-brimmed cap on his head.

She kept her arm straight but not stiff as she weighed her options. If she relaxed her string hand, the arrow would fly directly towards Ewen. If her brother thought she would willingly accept that weasel as her bridegroom, then he was mistaken. The squatty oaf might want to marry her, but perhaps he would feel differently if she embarrassed him to the point where he refused to take her.

Marriage was what was expected of any female by the age of twenty. But Isolde had always had other plans and her brother knew that as he pursued a marriage partner for her. Most likely it was because John had always been jealous of her abilities as a warrior, which far exceeded his own. Or, a more frightening thought was that John had no intention of allowing her to fight alongside his men, or in any Scottish army, no matter what their father had wanted.

Isolde frowned as she lessened the tension on her bow-string. Perhaps it was time for her to stop fighting the inevitable. She would never change her brother's mind. She'd been trying since her parents had died last year. If she wanted a different future than the one he had planned for her, it was time for her to strike out on her own and find another clan who would value her skills. With tension between the Scots and the English intensifying, perhaps even another branch of the Nicolson clan on the mainland might overlook her gender.

She'd considered pretending to be a man instead of a woman, but that could become problematic quickly if she were discovered. Nay, it was better to find a clan who would accept her for who she was. She was proud of her skills and abilities; there had to be someone else in Scotland who would be as well.

"John thought you might be hiding up here."

Isolde did not turn to look at her pregnant sister-in-law. "What do you want, Sarah?"

"I come bearing good news," Sarah said in a cheerful voice as she cupped her very round abdomen with her hands. "Your bridegroom has arrived."

Why had her brother allowed his wife to climb the tower steps when she was so heavy with child? The woman had only a few more days of her confinement until their first child would arrive. "He is not my bridegroom," Isolde said.

"If you loose that arrow, he will not be. But then again you won't be a bride either," Sarah said in an annoyingly sweet tone. "Your wedding will become a hanging instead."

Isolde lowered her bow and swivelled towards Sarah. "I was not going to kill him."

"It looked like you were going to do just that."

Isolde frowned. "I was only going to give Ewen MacPhee a reason to regret appearing here this day as I divested him of his hat."

Sarah's good humour faded. "You could have missed."

"I never miss," Isolde said with a lift of her chin.

"Your stubborn pride will be the end of you one day, Isolde." Sarah's lips pressed into a thin line. "John is trying to help see you settled. It is his responsibility to do so. He truly wants to see you promised before our child arrives."

"I want different things," Isolde said tartly.

Sarah shook her head. "Women do not have the luxury of wanting anything other than marriage and children, no matter how talented they are with a bow. It is your duty as the laird's sister to obey him. John has been more than fair with you. In fact, if you would come below with me, you would see that your brother is prepared to offer you a compromise."

Isolde frowned. "What kind of compromise?"

Sarah's features eased into a more sincere smile as she motioned towards the open doorway leading from the tower to the rooms below. "Come and see for yourself."

In silence, she and Sarah slowly walked down the stairs that curved inside the tower. Isolde kept hold of Sarah's arm as they descended to make certain she did not fall. The pace gave her plenty of time to observe the windows that were too narrow to slip through along the stairwell. Through the castle's open doorway, Isolde heard male voices. They were still too far away to make out the words. What kind of compromise awaited her in the courtyard? Her brother was not often charitable when it came to her. So she would be wise to temper her expectations. But she had to admit she was curious.

When they reached the bottom of the tower, Isolde opened the door for Sarah to pass through then stepped out onto the grassy area adjacent to the courtyard. The late-summer sunshine was only now burning through the mist that still lingered on the ground, making the scene before her seem a little unreal.

Seven of the men who had arrived earlier now remained near her brother. As she approached, they all turned to stare. Ewen smiled and punched the man beside him in the arm. "There she is, my soon-to-be bride." His deep voice resonated through the courtyard, setting Isolde's nerves on end. Instead of arguing, she glanced at her brother.

Sarah moved to her husband's side and whispered in his ear, Most likely telling him how she'd found Isolde on the tower. A frown of displeasure cut across John's face. "Were you about to slay one of these men?"

"I do not condone murder, Brother. But I will defend myself, if necessary, from you forcing me into wedlock."

"I have learned long ago that I cannot force you to do anything you do not wish to do. So, instead I have devised a test of your abilities that will determine your future for you." He turned towards the open area of the courtyard, which had been set with three stacks of hay and three targets made of coiled straw that were a great distance away. "Since you take great pride in your skill as an archer, I challenge you to best Ewen in hitting these targets. If you win, I will allow you to fight with my guards. If he wins, you will surrender your bow and arrow and marry him this very day."

Isolde stared at her brother in disbelief. Was he truly giving her a choice? Or at least a chance to decide her own fate? Or was this a trick of some sort? If she agreed, and didn't live up to her end of the competition, she would be married by the end of the day. Or was that what John hoped? That by agreeing, she would start to question her own abilities and fail?

Whatever may be, she didn't really have any other option. She had to compete, and she trusted her own skills to see her through. "I agree to your terms," she said without looking at Ewen.

"Then come." Her brother motioned for her to follow as he headed towards the castle. With the stone wall behind them, the entire courtyard lay before them. She would have to strike the targets from at least seven and seventy yards away. She'd done that before, but this time she would have to do it better than the man who now stood beside her.

In his hands, Ewen held a long bow, and his quiver held a number of arrows that were several inches longer than her arrows. While he strung his bow, the sound of footfalls coming from the castle doorway filled the air. Others from the castle had come to watch, alerted by their voices that something significant was happening outside.

Silence suddenly filled the courtyard as Ewen raised his bow and nocked an arrow. He gave Isolde a smug smile before he let the arrow fly, easily driving one arrow then another into the coiled straw, marking the target. "There. Best that," he said stepping aside.

All eyes were upon her as she lifted her bow, drew an arrow from her quiver, then concentrated on the target. His arrows had struck the target in the centre. She would have to hit the space between his arrow to best him.

She forced her arm to remain relaxed as she sighted the target and let first one arrow, then a second.

Her arrows hit the target. She didn't have to race down to the target to see that her strikes were directly above his arrows.

John and Sarah rushed to the target to inspect the shots. "It's a tie," John announced before moving back out of the way.

Ewen nodded, seeming pleased with that outcome. He moved to the left, in alignment with the second target. He took his time lining up his shot, then let his arrows fly in rapid succession once more. One arrow hit the target dead centre and the other arrow knocked the first from its placement. He'd shot both with exact precision.

A heaviness weighed Isolde down as she took her place and raised her bow. She'd proved herself time and again. To Father. To his master-at-arms. To at least half the men in the castle. And now she would have to prove herself yet again. She had to hit near dead centre twice, or her hopes of gaining her freedom from marriage might be at an end. Swallowing tightly, she drew the string of her bow back until it touched her lips and the middle of her chin. As she had a hundred times before, she let her arrow ease off the string. It arched at what seemed an impossibly slow pace, but as the arrow reached its arc it sped towards the target. Isolde held her breath even as she reached for a second arrow, sending it after the other. The first arrow hit right next to Ewen's arrow at the centre of the target. The second arrow hit right beside the first, setting all the arrows quivering at the impact.

Isolde lowered her bow as John moved to the target. Ewen frowned. Once John had finished his inspection, he turned to those gathered and announced, "Round two goes to Isolde."

"Well done," Ewen said, but the words hardly sounded like praise.

Even so, a swell of pride warmed Isolde's chest for a heartbeat before she tamped it down. She had to win this final round for her dreams to become reality—to prove once and for all she was worthy of fighting alongside any of them.

With a stern look on his face, Ewen moved to the third target. The crowd murmured in anticipation as he prepared for the final round. Once he brought his arrow up, silence descended over the courtyard. His arrow flew straight and true, burrowing into the target at the centre. His second arrow followed quickly, and hit the target right beside the other arrow. His smug grin reappeared. "Try to beat me now, if you can."

Ewen wasn't giving up without a fight. She had to best him once more with two perfectly aimed arrows. Again, those gathered conversed amongst themselves as Isolde lined up with the target. Ewen came to stand beside her.

"You're not worried about hitting the target, are you?" he asked in a snide tone.

He was trying to intimidate her with his presence. Well, it didn't matter. She would hit her target regardless.

The noise about them silenced, until Isolde could hear only the sound of her own breathing. She sighted the end of Ewen's arrow in the target and with a burst of confidence slowly released her grip. In the same instant, Ewen's foot came out and tapped hers, sending her arrow off target. Instant outrage filled her. In the span of a heartbeat, she plucked another arrow from her quiver and stepped farther away, letting the arrow fly, then another after that. But this time, Ewen lunged straight at her, knocking the third arrow in a wild arc, well away from the target. Isolde fell to the ground with a thump. Ewen fell on top of her.

"Get off me!" She pushed Ewen's big body away and wiggled out from under him before gaining her feet.

A cacophony of noise filled the courtyard—from jests that she had been beaten, to those protesting that Ewen had cheated. But two sounds rose above the others. A cry of distress sounded, then a second bellow of rage.

Isolde looked to where her brother and sister-in-law had stood next to the targets. Sarah lay upon the ground, clutching an arrow in her lower abdomen. John knelt beside her with an arrow protruding from his shoulder.

A cold chill came over Isolde. She twisted towards Ewen. "Look what your cheating has caused."

His features hardened. "I wasn't the one firing the arrows."

With disgust, she raced to John and Sarah, tossing the bow and quiver to the ground before dropping to her knees beside them. "What can I do? How can I help?"

"My baby. Please, someone help my baby."

Isolde reached for Sarah's hand as the pregnant woman groaned in pain.

Her brother's face contorted with rage and pain as he looked to Isolde. "You've done enough." He slapped her hand away. "Get away from Sarah. Get away from me. In fact, get out of this castle. You wanted your freedom. Take it. Leave with the clothes on your back. Nothing more. I never wish to see you again."

John tried to scoop Sarah up in his arms but when that failed because of his own injury, he motioned for one of his men to lift her instead. John followed behind as Sarah was carried to the castle. When Isolde accompanied them, John paused to rake her with another icy glare of hatred. "Get her out of here. And someone fetch the midwife."

"Nay!" One voice cut through the noise. "She has been wronged by a cheater. Do not force her to leave." Maribeth, Isolde's maid protested, coming to Isolde's side.

But her plea fell on deaf ears as her brother once again shouted, "You shot the arrows, Isolde. You threaten the life of my child. In turn, I will threaten your life by disowning you."

Isolde knew her brother was serious. She'd seen that look on his face when they were children and she'd bested him in competition. The thought gripped her around the throat as she fought to swallow. Quickly, she snapped up her quiver, slinging it over her shoulder, then her bow, and headed for the still-open gates. Without looking back, she raced across the drawbridge and into the wilderness beyond Scorrybreac Castle.

CLUTCHING HER BOW in her hand, Isolde ran. Dedication. Bravery. Daring. It had all been turned against her. All her dreams shattered about her with each footfall across the moors she knew so well.

She headed to the south, running from an invisible monster that would only follow her wherever she went. Ewen had cheated, but she would bear the burden of the events of this day. Her life as she knew it was over. All her dreams were dead.

Her breath caught in her throat as she pushed herself to run faster. Tears streaked from her eyes, caught up by the wind. She tripped, staggered, then went down hard on her knees. Her bow slipped from her hand. And in the next moment eight men in bright red coats surged forward, from out of nowhere. She'd been so distracted that she hadn't even noticed their approach. They grasped her by the hair, caught her by the sleeve, dug their nails into her flesh. "Where are you going in such a hurry?" A young soldier with auburn hair narrowed his gaze on her.

British soldiers. "Release me." Isolde struggled against their grip. "You've no right to detain me."

"We can do whatever we want, little lady," another young man at her elbow said as his mouth stretched into a brief, taunting smile.

Her heart pounded in her ears as she stretched her hand out, hoping she could touch the end of her bow. These men were too close to shoot with arrows, but she could bash them in the head with the wooden limb of her bow.

"Cease." A voice came from off to her right.

Isolde turned towards the sound, as the men holding her relaxed their grips, to see an older man in his forties holding a pistol in his hands. As he strode towards her, he lowered the weapon. "Bind her," he ordered his men. "Then take her to my tent."

Isolde continued to fight as they bound her hands before her. She kept struggling even when they lifted her onto her feet. When she refused to move on her own, they lifted her by the arms and carried her still writhing and kicking into the tent she had been too distressed to see before. Inside the shelter, they forced her onto a wooden crate then left as the man with the pistol entered.

He set the pistol near the door and studied her through narrowed eyes. "Were you going to attack us with your weapon?"

She remained silent.

"It seems rather imbecilic for Laird Nicolson to send a single archer to defeat his enemy."

At the mention of her brother's name, Isolde tensed.

The man's eyes narrowed. "So you know the laird of whom I speak?"

She remained motionless as she returned the man's piercing gaze. Her brother had suffered enough at her hands today.

"I mean you no harm," he said, holding his palms out towards her.

She lifted her bound hands. "These lashings at my wrists

say otherwise."

He arched a brow as he came towards her. "If you promise to behave yourself, I will release you." He pulled a dagger from his belt but hesitated until she nodded her consent.

With a single cut, he released her. "I am Lieutenant Cornelius Collins from one of the companies that make up the twenty-ninth regiment." He offered her a bow. "My men and I have been charged with obtaining information about Laird Nicolson and other rebel lairds in this area."

"What does that have to do with me?"

He studied her, not as a man eyed a woman but in judgement of her dedication, her intentions. "Much, if you are as clever as you are brave. You tried to take on eight of my men with one bow. I find that interesting. And since we saw you running from the direction of Scorrybreac Castle, I'd venture to guess you are somehow associated with the laird and his clan."

She swallowed roughly. She could not reveal the nature of her association or the banishment she'd been dealt without making herself even more vulnerable to the lieutenant and his men.

"Nothing to say?" Lieutenant Collins frowned. "You are in a precarious situation as a female out of your castle alone, with no one to protect you."

Isolde bristled at the unveiled threat. "I can protect myself."

"I'm counting on that." Lieutenant Collins's lips pulled

up into a cunning smile. "I need someone like you on my side."

Isolde narrowed her gaze on the Englishman. Anything he wanted her to do could not be good for the Scots. "What do you mean?"

"You will spy on your countrymen for me. Inform me of their allegiances and their movements."

On edge already, she flinched. "Why would I do such a thing?"

Lieutenant Collins's features hardened as he turned his dagger towards her. "Because if you don't, I will arrest your brother, Laird Nicolson, for crimes against the crown."

"He's done nothing of the sort. I will testify on his behalf that he's been a loyal servant to the crown."

"And who will the English courts believe, the sister of a man with Jacobite ties, or one of their own military officers?" His smile turned cruel.

If this man knew she was John's sister, then the English had been spying on the Nicolson clan. Isolde drew a tense breath, let it go between parted lips. The lieutenant meant what he said. Did she really have any choice?

For the first time that day Isolde saw that her brother's plan to marry her off might have had merit. At least she would have been safe even if it was with Ewen MacPhee. Isolde looked at the lieutenant's large, powerful hands and the lethal dagger in them. She met his amber gaze. "What would you have me do?"

She had no choice but to cooperate. Yet she would not send her countrymen to their deaths in this game of espionage. There had to be another way, and eventually she would find it.

CHAPTER TWO

Isle of Skye, Scotland
Friday, November 16th, 1742

ORRICK MACLEOD RODE his horse away from Dunvegan Castle to the east, towards the flat-topped peaks of Healabhal Beag and Healabhal Mór, known to those on the isle as MacLeod's Tables. The chill morning air brushed against his cheeks as he pushed his horse into a faster gait. The cold last night and the chill this morning meant it was imperative that he find the little girl who'd gone missing after the MacQueens raided the village of Orbost the day before.

When the MacLeods arrived at the village after receiving word that the village was under attack, they were too late to drive the attackers away. They'd already done their damage to the small village on the outskirts of MacLeod territory. It was another strike from the clans who supported the MacDonalds that signalled another escalation of the battle between the MacDonalds and the MacLeods.

Alastair, the MacLeod clan leader and Orrick's brother, had tried desperately to negotiate peace between the Mac-

Donalds and the MacLeods and their allied clans. The Scots had far more pressing matters to contend with now that English regiments patrolled the Highlands. But with each clan attack on the villages nearby, any kind of peace agreement between the clans seemed more unlikely. Eventually the antagonism between the MacDonalds and the MacLeods would become a full-out war. The thought sent a shiver of fear down Orrick's spine. To win such a conflict would take every warrior the MacLeods had in their army.

There had been a time when all three of the MacLeod triplets had fought in battles alongside their father. They were a fighting force feared amongst not only the other isle clans but also the English. But when their father had sustained a head wound years ago and he'd transformed from a fair man to a brutal warrior overnight, Orrick and his brothers had refused to fight alongside their father. Then when he'd murdered their mother, the triplets had left Dunvegan and their father behind.

Tormod and Orrick had gone to the West Indies, seeking to earn their fortunes so they might have independence from their father. While Tormod had embraced the experience, Orrick had discovered that the senseless loss of life ate away at his soul. He had killed so many men who were fathers and brothers, all in the name of British expansion. And when he could fight for domination over the oppressed no longer, he and Tormod had switched sides, fighting instead for Spain.

But even that failed to help. They were still taking the lives of men who were only fighting because they were ordered to do so by their commanders. With each day and each battle, it became harder and harder for Orrick to lift his sword, until instead of fighting, he found a way to help those who were being slaughtered and enslaved. Orrick had only been back at Dunvegan for six months, and he'd not been able to lift his weapon even to help fight against the MacDonalds, their clan's enemy.

Orrick forced back the memories of the West Indies and his inability to be the warrior he was once. Today, all his thoughts and all his skills had to be focused on finding the lost child.

The girl, who was said to be an orphan, hadn't been missed until nightfall. Orrick and his brothers had done a search in the darkness for several hours, but had failed to find her. At first light, Alastair and Tormod had headed west to search the shoreline. Callum and Graeme had headed north towards the rivers and streams, while Orrick had headed off alone to search the vast territory to the east. Other members of the household searched closer to the castle grounds.

Though the situation was urgent, Orrick took a moment to take in the spectacular landscape surrounding his home. According to legend, the flat-topped summits before him were created after a visit from Saint Columba to Skye. The holy man was not well received by the then chief of the MacLeods, who lived in a fort on the shores of Loch Bracadale. While Saint Columba preached a sermon about messengers from the Lord not having a place to lay their heads, the skies blackened and the ground shook, culminating in a mighty crash. When the world around them settled, those at the sermon left the church to discover the tops of two local mountains had been struck off, creating a bed for Saint Columba to sleep on and a table for him to dine at. The story was just one of many involving the MacLeods of Skye.

Right now, it was a little girl who needed a warm place to sleep and a table to eat at. Orrick could only imagine how scared the four-year-old child was out there, alone, in the wilderness. He encouraged his horse, Phoenix, into a quicker pace while he kept his eyes trained on the tall grass for anything out of the ordinary. The girl had been described as blond, and wearing a brown dress, which would make finding her that much harder since she blended in with the landscape. He would find her regardless. He had to.

FROM HIGH ATOP the summit of Healabhal Beag, Isolde took in the breathtaking view of the Black Cuillins and Loch Bharscavaig. Much had happened to her since she'd left her brother's castle fourteen months ago. She'd worked for Lieutenant Collins for two months. After feeding him useless information for weeks, he'd once again threatened her brother and she'd been forced to reveal the many late-night trips to Orbost where Dugald MacTavish met with Sir James Campbell of Auchinbreck. She'd followed the man to his meeting location and had overheard plans to raise men in favour of Bonnie Prince Charlie and the Jacobite cause. Two days later, both men were arrested and imprisoned at Dumbarton Castle.

At the news, her body had gone numb and the breath had stilled in her lungs. If a man was measured by his actions, then surely a woman was as well. She had betrayed her country. She had betrayed her people. The lieutenant had threatened her brother's life if she didn't cooperate. But she knew from experience her brother was a man to be reckoned with. At least from Lieutenant Collins's constant threats, she knew her brother had not succumbed to the arrow she'd hit him with. Sarah and her child he'd never mentioned and Isolde feared the worst. Her brother had survived then, and John would continue to do so in the future because in order to protect him, Isolde had had no choice but to disappear, to vanish somewhere no one would ever find her.

And she had. For the past year, she'd made a life for herself in the wilderness surrounding MacLeod's Tables. Healabhal Beag was the higher of the two peaks that marked the edge of the MacLeods' vast territory to the east. In all the time since she'd lived at the base of the mountain, no one had ventured anywhere near her since she'd escaped the

English. Her days as an informant were at an end. Now, she focused on survival.

She'd only taken twelve arrows with her from Scorrybreac. Though using those twelve, she'd taught herself how to keep the arrowheads sharp, how to replace the shafts using tree branches and fish scales to smooth the wood, and she'd learned how to fletch the arrows with feathers from the birds she hunted for food. As of late, she'd also started experimenting with making her own arrowheads from slate like ancient people used to before they discovered copper and steel. Every time she used an arrow, she made certain to retrieve it, as she would today.

Isolde surveyed the land before her with her bow in her hand and quiver at her back. She'd come to hunt. She needed to find something other than the rabbits, squirrels, and birds that had sustained her all summer and fall, if she were to make it through another Highland winter in isolation. She'd climbed partially up Healabhal Beag to determine where the Scottish red deer were grazing this morning, as well as survey any English activity in the vicinity. Lieutenant Collins's company had turned to the south a few months after her escape.

She'd seen no signs of them or any other troops since the leaves had fallen from the trees. No doubt they'd moved on to warmer climes for the winter, which suited her needs perfectly. She was free to hunt and live without constant fear of discovery. But she needed to find food if she were to be able to remain hidden in these hills. If she could fell one red deer from the wild herd, she would be well supplied with meat for the coming months.

Isolde inhaled the icy scent of the earth as it mixed with early morning sky. Overhead dark clouds gathered, threatening snowfall later in the day. She had to hurry and accomplish her task before the snow fell and the animals sought shelter from the cold. Bringing her gaze back to the landscape before her, Isolde caught movement to the west. A large herd, with several males bearing five- to six-pointed antlers, grazed amongst numerous females on the grass, willowherb, and brambles that still remained after last night's frost. Having achieved her goal, Isolde started her descent, hoping the animals would remain while she hiked down from the summit over the next couple of hours.

She was nearly to the base of the mountain when she stopped. An odd feeling came over her, something she hadn't felt in months. She swallowed. It almost felt like someone or something was watching her.

She looked about her. Nothing moved and only the usual sounds of the wind and the sea in the distance came to her. She shrugged off the sensation and continued her climb down when another ripple of movement caught her attention. Something much smaller than the red deer surged through the tall grass. She stopped and concentrated on the sight until she could make out the unmistakable stripes of a family of badgers. She groaned as she hurried down the remaining slope. Badgers could complicate her hunt if she didn't hurry.

Silently stalking through the grass with her bow at her side, Isolde heard a noise off to her right. She froze, concentrating on the sound. Careful to make no noise, she reached for a bow from her quiver and strung it. Blood pounded in her ears. Had she missed something while surveying the territory from above? She was prepared to fight the English single-handed if she must. For she was done being their spy.

She'd practised her skill with a bow and arrow every day, despite the memories of her last day at Scorrybreac. She knew her brother lived, but what about her sister-in-law and the babe? She'd not been able to find any information on either of them since she left.

Forcing the memories aside, Isolde crouched down, pulling her handmade hooded fur cloak tight around her, not wanting to alert anyone that she was closing in as she moved carefully towards the sound. The noise came again, louder this time. She was close. Preparing to strike, Isolde pulled the string of her bow back and stood, ready to fire. And came face to face with a man. He was not English, but Scottish.

Orrick MacLeod.

Her breath caught at the sight of him. He was taller than she remembered, and thick with muscle. He wore leather armour across his chest and upper arms. And in his hands, he held a bow with an arrow pointed directly at her head.

He stared at her, breathing hard. Orrick's brow rose from

what she imagined was a persistent furrow, giving him a look of surprise. "You are not a wee little lass." His eyes sharpened on her face. "What are you? A witch?"

A wee lass? A witch? What was he talking about? Had the youngest of the MacLeod triplets gone mad since she'd last seen him six years ago? She'd been a lass and he a lean-muscled, tall lad when they'd met at the Highland games. He'd smiled at her for a heartbeat until the other lads nearby had teased her about her quiver and bow.

"Girls can't compete."

"Girls can't shoot an arrow."

"Go home to your mama." The boys had taunted her. Orrick had joined in their laughter and turned away.

"What are you doing on MacLeod land?" he asked, his voice hard. His dark brown hair caught the wind, lending a certain fierceness to his stony jaw. "Are you human or beast?"

Over the last fourteen months, her clothing had deteriorated and she'd been forced to create a full-length cloak from rabbit pelts sewn together with sinew. And granted, her hair had become a wild tangle despite her attempts to tame the thickness with a comb she'd fashioned from animal bone. But she was clean. She bathed almost daily in the nearby creek during the warmer days. Now, as the days grew cold, she limited her bathing to sunny days despite the frigid chill that often hung in the air.

He stared into her face as though trying to see past her outward appearance. "Who are you? What are you doing out here alone?"

"I'm . . ." The word caught in her throat. It had been a year since she had spoken a word to anyone. She tried again. "I'm hunting." The words crackled from a throat that felt raw. How had speaking become such an effort?

His eyes narrowed. "Hunting on another man's property is punishable by hanging."

She frowned. "You'd have to . . . catch me . . . first."

Orrick's lips thinned and then eased as if no longer seeing her as a major threat. "There is something familiar about you."

"What did you mean . . . about a wee lass?" Her throat was still raw, but she forced the words past the ache. "Why would she . . . be out here?" she asked, straining to hold her bowstring taut for such a long period of time.

"We could spend the morning shooting at each other until one of us is dead or out of arrows, or you could help me find the little girl who disappeared from Orbost after the MacQueens raided the village yesterday."

She stared down the length of her arrow into the rich brown of Orrick's eyes. As they stared at each other, she allowed her gaze to slide along the solid jaw that was covered by a day's growth of beard, across his straight nose, to his cheekbones where a thin white line showed a scar.

His brows were bent and his full lips were parted. After a long moment, he exhaled and lowered his bow. He returned his arrow to his quiver. "What say you to a truce?"

He offered her a smile. She forced herself to breathe evenly and to battle against the odd sensation that tingled through her body. It had been a while since she'd been this close to another human being, let alone a handsome male. She lowered her bow and stepped back. "Let's find the girl."

CHAPTER THREE

O RRICK STARED AT the creature before him. At first sight, she appeared like a wild animal with soft grey fur covering her blond hair. From beneath the hood of her cloak shone piercing blue eyes. The fear he'd seen in those eyes when he'd risen up over her had faded, replaced by both determination and strength.

How had she ended up out here? Alone? Judging by her appearance, she'd been out in the wilderness for quite some time. The clothing beneath her cloak was ragged, and instead of slippers or boots, she wore lengths of hide tied about her feet to protect them from the cold.

She drew back the hood of her cloak to reveal a tangle of wild blond hair. "You think the child is near here?" the wild woman asked in a voice that seemed stronger now.

The morning light played off the gentle contours of her cheeks and seemed to highlight her full lips. Despite her dishevelled state, her skin was clean, radiant almost. "Not long ago, I found small footprints leading this way," Orrick said. "From the freshness of the last tracks, I know she's close."

The woman nodded. "You take the north and east. I will search the south and west."

They both turned from each other just as a grunting sound filled the air followed by chittering then a snarl. A heartbeat later a shrill scream sounded and the snarling grew louder. Birds hiding in the tall grass took flight, and the combined bellows of several red deer sounded close by.

"That's a badger," the woman said, turning back towards Orrick.

She raced past him towards a thrashing sound. Orrick hesitated for a moment as panic surged through him. He clutched his bow in his hands and reached for an arrow from his quiver, but he couldn't bring himself to set the arrow in place as shame flooded his limbs. All his past failures rose up before him and he saw the unseeing eyes of the men he had killed, staring back at him. Orrick had taken the lives of men simply for fighting on the opposite side from his men who were defending their homeland from British expansion.

The woman, however, did not hesitate. Orrick pushed the memories aside and followed. They broke through to a clearing to see an adult badger with a little girl's leg clamped tightly in its jaws. The badger whipped its black-and-white striped head back and forth, while the little girl shrieked in terror. Why was the badger behaving so savagely? The animals generally only attacked when threatened or provoked. No matter what had happened, the situation was dire.

Instead of raising her own weapon, the wild woman

pulled her cloak around her and threw her body to the ground, sliding towards both animal and child. She reached for the little girl and engulfed her in her cloak, startling the badger enough for the animal to release the child's leg.

It didn't take long for the badger to recover from its shock. With an angry snarl, it leapt towards the two females coiled together and, finding the exposed flesh of the wild woman's arm, the animal latched on once more, screaming its displeasure.

Orrick raised his bow and nocked his arrow. His blood pounded in his ears. Taking the life of an animal was different from killing a man. And yet he couldn't seem to loose his fingers from the bow. His stomach clenched. He had to take the shot to save the woman and child.

But the woman and child faded from view. *Instead, he and his men advanced on the British. They'd been given the order to charge even though hundreds of them would be killed in the initial volley. Down the hill they went, into the valley below.*

The acrid scent of powder and black clouds enveloped him and the others as they continued down the slope. Beneath his feet he could feel the bodies that had fallen, smelled the metallic scent of blood, heard the shouting of the enemy, the cries of the fallen even as a new barrage of flame and balls came at them. The targe on his arm warded away the balls with a screech of metal on metal. He charged and sliced through a crimson uniform jacket, the shirt beneath, then the flesh of an Englishman. It mattered not. All that mattered was staying alive as he took the lives of others.

Drenched in sweat, Orrick came back to the moment. His heart pounded. His breath rasped in his throat as he expelled air and released the memory from his thoughts. He was whole. Unharmed. Unbloodied. Safe. Yet he was not alone as he usually was when the memories overcame him.

The woman. His body chilled as the sweat dried in the morning air. He had to help the woman. He fixed on her position, watching as she coiled her body around that of the child. Her movements dislodged the badger from her arm, its face bloodstained. The angry animal backed away. Its body puffed up and all its fur stood on end as it continued to snarl and hiss.

The animal looked from the pile of furs to Orrick, even though he had lowered his bow, and it hissed again. It did not charge. Instead, as though sensing imminent danger, the badger slowly crept backwards towards the grass. The animal headed farther and farther away from the three of them, until only the sound of the child softly sobbing could be heard.

Orrick steeled himself and hurried to the two females.

He knelt beside the woman and brushed the hair aside that had fallen across her face. "Are you injured?" She had tucked her arm inside her pelts, hiding it from view.

The woman opened her eyes and stared up at him. Her face pinched in pain.

"May I pick you and the child up? My horse is not far from here." He let out a shrill whistle that Phoenix would recognise as a command to come to his master. When the woman remained silent, he asked again, "Are you injured?"

"My arm is bleeding," the woman said. "I do not know about the child." Slowly she unfurled herself until he could see the little girl bundled within her fur cloak.

Orrick breathed a soft sigh that she was still alive. He gently placed a finger beneath the child's chin and brought her gaze to his. The little girl continued to sob. "Does anything pain you?"

"My leg," she said on a soft sob.

Orrick released the child's face and, as gently as possible, scooped the girl into his arms. He could see blood staining her shredded stockings. "I'll need to take you back to Dunvegan quickly."

The woman stood, further tucking her arm beneath her cloak so that Orrick could not see the extent of her injuries. "My campsite is closer."

He nodded and turned away as his horse approached. He set the girl on the saddle then turned to the woman. "You should ride with the child. I'll walk."

She hesitated for a moment then nodded. The look in her eyes said she trusted him or was too injured to object.

As she approached, the horse tossed his head and pinned his ears back, but remained steady while she climbed onto his back. Did his horse sense danger from this woman? Or could it sense her injuries? The smell of blood always made Phoenix unsettled. Perhaps that was why the animal acted as he did. For in her current state, the woman was harmless, but just to be certain, he reached up and grasped the end of her bow, removing it from her shoulder.

She tensed and gripped the bow, stopping his movements.

"It will take all your focus to keep you and the girl on the horse."

After a moment she nodded and allowed him to take the weapon. Once they were settled, Orrick gathered the reins and patted Phoenix's head, trying to calm the animal. "Which direction do we head?" he asked the woman.

"To the east. Towards the base of Healabhal Beag." The woman flinched and pain etched the corners of her mouth as Phoenix set in motion, but she held her cries of pain in check even as the little girl continued to sob within the curl of the woman's arms.

As they journeyed, the little girl's crying turned to sniffles. The relative quiet, while welcome, only intensified the questions racing through Orrick's mind. Why was the woman out here alone hunting? How long had she been on her own in the wilderness? Who was she?

They'd gone nearly a quarter of a mile when she swayed in the saddle as though the strength that had sustained her until now had suddenly left her. Orrick reached up to steady her, placing a hand at her trim waist. At his touch she stiffened and righted herself. "You were about to fall from the horse," he explained as he withdrew his hand.

"We are almost there." She pointed into the distance. It

took Orrick a moment to realise what he was looking at. At first, it looked like a small gathering of sycamore trees that had lost their leaves for the winter. But then he saw the lashings around them and the unusual tilt from their base. When they came closer, he saw a darkness behind those trees that was the opening of a cave. He would have passed by it if he hadn't been directed to it, for it was that well hidden.

Orrick led Phoenix into an overhang at the opening of the cave before he stopped. He reached up to take the child from the woman's arms, carrying the child inside the cave. A torch glowed in the depths, lighting an interior that was deeper than he'd thought. This cave would hold at least twenty men. How had she found such a thing when he never had, having ridden across this territory all his life?

He set the bows he carried against the wall before setting the child down on what could only be the woman's bed. It was a pile of rabbit pelts that had been sewn together to create a coverlet that rested atop a pile of feathers and moss to create a downy pillow of warmth and softness. While the girl nestled into the fur, Orrick returned to the cave's opening to find that the woman had already dismounted. Her face was pale and she swayed on her feet.

Orrick grabbed his saddle bag, then took her arm, leading her into the cave. Once inside, she pulled away and headed to a ledge that looked cut into the side of the rock. There, she withdrew a large bladder and handed it to him. "Bring the girl to the table where we can flush out her wounds with this water before I sew them together. I have a salve to keep them from putrefying and pounded tree bark we can use for bandages."

He turned to look at the handmade, sturdy table and single chair she pointed to. He did as directed and gathered the child, then laid her across the wooden surface. He pulled back the remains of the girl's frayed stocking to reveal two deep gashes in her flesh. He could see the bone beneath the top laceration, but it appeared that the bleeding had ceased, meaning her bleeding was from the surface wounds and not something deeper and far more dangerous. "What can I do? How can I help?" he asked.

"Flush the wounds, then go start a fire in the pit near the entrance of the cave. Everything you need is there."

He did as she asked, and when he returned a short while later, the woman had sewn the open gashes on the child's leg together in a row of neat and tidy stitches. The child had only cried out a few times. Obviously the woman was an experienced seamstress. Orrick frowned as he watched her spread a thick salve across the child's leg. Was his first thought about the woman correct? Was she a witch?

"What are you doing?" he asked in an accusatory tone as he stepped beside the girl and bent to smell the salve. "What kind of witchery is this?"

The sweet-smelling salve also had a hint of heather. He touched it and brought the sticky ointment to his lips, tasting it ever so lightly. "Honey?" He turned his gaze to hers.

"Honey has many healing properties."

He stepped back. "I apologise for jumping to conclusions. You are . . ." He paused, trying to find the right word. Mysterious, intriguing, a little frightening. "A surprise."

"I have been called worse." She shrugged and returned to her ministrations. When she finished with the honey, she wrapped the little girl's leg in a thin bandage of sorts. She'd said she had created it from pounded tree bark. "How did you learn all of this?" He pointed to the bark and the honey.

"Necessity."

His frown increased. "How long have you been out here?"

She shrugged. "I lost track a long while ago. Now I just watch the seasons change. This is my second winter."

"Over a year?" Orrick's gaze centred on her face. "Your clan has not come looking for you?"

She turned away. "I have no family. I have no one."

The words echoed through the silence of the cave and brought a tightness to Orrick's throat. He knew what it felt like to be so alone. He'd had that same experience in the West Indies even though he'd been surrounded by others. "You do not need to remain that way. Come back to Dunvegan with me."

She turned to face him again but instead of pain, fury brightened her blue eyes. "Nay. I can make my own way in this world."

Orrick looked about the sparsely furnished cave. She only had items she had created for herself from the surrounding area. Somehow she had managed to fashion a life for herself from nothing even though she resided upon MacLeod clan lands. "It was not my intent to upset you with such an invitation. Other things are far more important, such as letting me take a look at your wounds. I don't sew as well as you, but I can seal your wounds with my dagger."

She pulled her cloak more tightly around her. "There is no need. You should take the child back to her parents so they will worry no longer."

Why was she so reluctant to let him see her wounds? "The child has no parents. Only a foster family who did not notice her absence until hours after the attack on their village."

At talk of her family, or lack thereof, the girl started crying again. Her soft sobs echoed in the silence of the cavern.

The woman in pelts moved towards the bedside. "Poor lamb."

"Her name is Emlyn."

The woman sat at the bedside and gently brushed the matted strands of the child's hair from her cheeks. "Your parents named you 'brave, noble warrior.' Perhaps they knew you would one day be called upon to rise up against all odds."

The woman shifted her gaze back to Orrick. "You must take her back with you to Dunvegan immediately. See that she gets the care she needs in order to survive this ordeal and live up to her name."

Orrick kept his gaze steady. "You are very good at ordering me around."

She averted her gaze from his. "My apologies. I am simply trying to do what is best for Emlyn."

"What about you? You are injured as well. I won't take her back unless the both of you come with me. Emlyn will need someone to attend her."

"I am sure there are many women at the castle who can care for her better than I ever could."

He widened his stance and crossed his arms over his chest, holding his ground. "I'm not leaving without you."

"Your horse will make better time if you ride instead of walk the many miles back to the castle." The woman stood. "Take the girl and forget about me."

Before Orrick knew what she would do, she came directly at him, and going low as she had with the badger, whacked him on the back of his knees, forcing him to topple forward. As he tried to maintain his balance, she slipped past him and out of the cave.

Orrick turned to follow, but by the time he reached the cave's entrance, all signs of her had vanished. The world around him was as still and as quiet as the large flakes of snow now falling from the sky. He stepped outside the cave and searched the ground, looking for some trace of the woman's direction. Other than a small drop of blood near the entrance of the cave, he found no other signs of her presence.

He frowned into the ever-increasing snowfall. She obviously did not want to come back to Dunvegan with him, but she was still injured whether she wanted to admit it or not. And he did feel partially responsible for her injuries. If he had killed the badger immediately upon seeing it mauling the child, her injuries could have been avoided.

"God's blood!"

She had wanted him to forget her. That would be impossible. For she had made a rather memorable impression on him. Even now, the image of her delicate face framed in a halo of wild, blond hair, came to him. There was something intriguing about the woman who had stood before him with an arrow aimed at his chest as bravely and as steadfast as any male.

With a harsh sigh, Orrick turned around and headed into the depths of the cave once more. She'd given him no choice but to take Emlyn back to the castle before the weather worsened, and to call off the search party. But that did not mean he could not return.

He would come back for the mysterious woman and learn more about her. She seemed familiar to him, and yet he could not figure out where they might have met. Perhaps it would come to him on the journey back to Dunvegan.

He did not know her name, he knew next to nothing about her, but he was certain all his thoughts would be of her until he returned to this cave.

CHAPTER FOUR

P EEKING OUT THROUGH the camouflaged hide she'd created near the entrance of her cave, Isolde watched as he rode into the distance. Though she hadn't seen Orrick or his brothers since the Highland games six years ago, she'd always been able to tell which of the three had been Orrick. There was something different about the way he held himself that stood out from his brothers. When he looked at her, his smile had been a little brighter, his eyes gentler. At least they had until his friends had turned him against her.

With a frown, Isolde reined in her thoughts. Only when she was certain Orrick could not see her did she emerge and head back into the cave. She warmed herself by the fire he had left burning at the cave's entrance as she tried to determine what to do next.

It would be wise for her to abandon the cave and move to a second location she had started to dig out of the hillside at the base of Healabhal Mór. But as she stared at the flames, they wavered before her eyes. Her injury was worse than she'd let on. Carefully she pushed her blood-soaked cloak back to reveal the damage to her left arm. The badger's sharp teeth had shredded what remained of her sleeve and had dug into the flesh beneath. A V-shaped tear of skin and muscle hung loose from the upper part of her arm, and blood continued to seep from inside. The injury would make holding her bow far more difficult, but she would worry about that at another time. Right now, she had to stop the bleeding.

Isolde reached for the *sgian-dubh* tucked inside her handmade boots and held the blade in the centre of the bluish-red flames. The only way to stop the bleeding and hope for any kind of repair to her arm would be to seal the wound herself, then pray she didn't pass out from the pain before she was through.

Once that task was complete, then she would leave her cave behind. She could not risk the MacLeod finding her again, for his sake and for her own. Associating with her in any way was simply too dangerous when the English returned. And they would come back to the Highlands, of that Isolde was certain. There were still too many clan chiefs who had not pledged their allegiance to the king, including the MacLeods.

As she waited for the blade to heat, she shivered, once again feeling as though someone watched her. She left the fire and moved to the entrance of the cave but could find nothing out of the ordinary. Attributing her unease to her condition, she returned to the fire. When the blade glowed red, Isolde wrapped the grip with leather, then inhaling deeply set the hot knife against her flesh, forcing the torn skin back into place as it seared under the metal. Isolde cried out, the sound echoing through the empty cave. She forced herself to continue to hold the blade against her skin as the flames danced on the cave walls, writhing and swirling until she realised it wasn't the flames moving but herself. She drew another deep breath, her back stiffening as she returned the blade to the flames. The other side of the wound needed cauterising as well.

This time when the blade glowed hot, her hand shook as she brought the weapon up to her partially sealed wound. The scent of burning flesh assaulted her nostrils and turned her stomach as she laid the metal against her wound. Agonising pain seared through her. She bit the insides of her cheeks until she tasted blood in her mouth. *Only a few moments more.*

This time when the walls before her swayed, she allowed herself to topple to the ground and let the darkness that threatened engulf her.

———————

WHEN ORRICK REACHED Dunvegan Castle, he left the care of the little girl to Gwendolyn, Alastair's wife; Fiona, Tormod's wife; and his sister Rowena before riding to the west, finding his brother and calling off the search. This day would have a happy end because they'd found the missing child. It would have a happier end if he could convince the woman in the cave to come back home with him.

As he rode back towards where he'd left the woman, he wondered who she was. She'd said she'd been in the wilderness for over a year. If there were any stories about women gone missing from their clans, he and his brothers would not have heard them because they'd returned to the Isle of Skye only three months prior. So much had happened to them since then that they'd barely had time to settle into what some might call a routine. The chaos seemed to continue with events like yesterday's attack on Orbost, their issues with the MacDonalds, and the threat of English invasion. He doubted the MacLeods would settle into domestic bliss anytime soon.

The English patrols had ended for the season, but they would return, and when they did, who knew what the enemy would do to an unprotected woman. Orrick's lips quirked at the memory of the woman who had challenged him with her arrow. She was far from helpless, but she would be better protected amongst others. Perhaps then he could determine who she was and return her to her clan.

His brothers would once again chastise him for taking responsibility for the entire world, but it was who he was. He cared about the people who were caught up in the acts of war more than the war itself. His time in the West Indies had devolved into that very thing when Orrick realised he could no longer take lives, even those of the enemy.

He wanted to help others not destroy them. And so he had. He'd spent all his time and his ill-gained profits to usher families in the villages where they fought to safety. He rescued captured natives who would be sold as slaves from the ships that would take them to unfamiliar parts of the world. And he provided the funds they needed to start their new lives. He'd come back to Dunvegan no richer than when he'd left.

Now that he was home, it was time to focus on what came next. Third sons could choose between the law, the cloth, or the sword. The sword wasn't an option for him, and the other two held no appeal. Even if they did, the English restricted who passed the bar or was ordained to those whose clan leaders pledged their allegiance to the king. Something Alastair refused to do. His brothers supported that decision even if it made life more complicated for Tormod, Orrick, and Callum.

Despite the challenges, Orrick was lucky. He had a place to live, surrounded by others who loved and supported him, whether he could join in their battles or not. The woman in the cave had no one. Or so it appeared. He intended to change that.

When he approached the well-hidden cave once more, he slid from Phoenix's back and allowed the horse to graze on the blades of grass that peeked out from the fresh snowfall. Orrick studied the area. There were no footsteps in the snow to suggest the woman had left the cave—or any indication that she had returned from wherever she'd been hiding. Uncertain what he would find within the cave, Orrick stepped under the overhang and peered inside. The fire he'd started had died down, leaving the opening of the cave in darkness. When his eyes adjusted to the lack of light, it was then that he saw her lying on the ground. Was she dead? Had she bled out while he'd been gone because she'd refused to let him look at her wounds?

He rushed to her side and rolled her onto her back. "Please don't be dead," he said softly while searching her neck with his fingers for some sign that her life force still pulsed inside her.

She bolted upright at his touch as if she'd been sleeping and he'd thrown a bucket of cold water on her. She raised a fist that bore a *sgian-dubh* and aimed it at his heart.

He gripped her hand to stop the thrust and twisted until the blade fell from her fingers. Instead of settling down, she slugged him in the cheek with her other hand. "Unhand me, you churlish rogue."

She pulled back to hit him again, but Orrick gripped her wrist. "You're safe. I am not here to harm you."

Her gaze focused and a look of surprise widened her eyes. Surprise and a terrible sadness. "You came back."

"I said I would." The tension in her body relaxed and Orrick released her wrist. The scent of burning flesh hit him just then and he shifted his gaze from her face to her exposed upper arm where black charred flesh had replaced what was once a gaping wound. "That badger really lashed into your arm." A surge of guilt coiled in his chest. He should have killed the animal before it had attacked her.

She reached for her pelted cloak and pulled it across her arm, hiding the damage from his view. "Is Emlyn safe?"

"She is being cared for. Now you need someone to care for you. Please let me take you back to Dunvegan. You might have sealed your wound, but you need a healer to make certain it does not become putrid."

"The honey—"

"You used the last of it on Emlyn," Orrick interrupted. "It will take someone truly gifted in the art of healing to make certain you can use your bow as you did before."

The woman straightened her arm, as though testing to see if she could still hold her bow, then winced with pain. The sadness in her eyes shifted to fear. "Without my bow, I am nothing."

"Then come back to Dunvegan where a healer can make certain you will still have full use of your arm."

Her features shuttered. "I will not be your prisoner."

Orrick stood and held out his hand. "You will be free to leave whenever you desire." At her continued hesitation he added, "I promise."

"Why?" She tilted her head, her startling blue eyes curious and suspicious.

He shrugged. Why he wanted her to come back with him was a question he had to answer for himself as much as her. "It feels like the right thing to do."

"You appear to be a warrior, and yet you would base your actions on a feeling? That seems very out of character."

"I've spent the past five years of my life fighting for causes that were not my own in the West Indies, and because of that I lost myself. Now that I have returned home, I'm not certain what I'm supposed to do. I am no longer the man I was when I left." Why was he telling a perfect stranger his deepest fears when he had not admitted such to his own family? Perhaps it was easier because she was unknown to him.

She gave him a weary smile. "What are any of us who are survivors supposed to do when our lives shift beneath us?"

That question had haunted him since his return to Dunvegan. "I had hoped to cultivate peace, put away my sword, settle down." He studied her face. This woman was unfamiliar, but on some level she was also familiar. Perhaps because she appeared as lost and alone as he was. "You seem to have survived something horrible that has happened to you. Perhaps you want the same things?"

A glimmer of hope reflected in her eyes before it died a heartbeat later, replaced by sadness once more. "The English will allow neither of us to put away our weapons anytime soon."

"Perhaps. But they are not on Skye at the moment. It is safe for you to let down your guard for a short while until you heal. Are you willing to allow yourself that time?"

At first he thought she would maintain her silence, but then she sighed. "I'm no use to anyone, including myself, until I heal and can use my bow and arrows again."

He stretched out his hand once more. "Then come with me."

She frowned at his hand, but eventually she shifted her weight onto her feet, took his hand, and stood. "I will only stay until my arm heals." She pulled her fingers from his.

Perhaps if they were no longer strangers she would trust him more. "We've not been formally introduced. I am Orrick MacLeod. And you are?"

"You may call me Isolde."

He frowned. "You have no clan?"

"None that would claim me."

He winced as he recognised how much pain lay under her words. Perhaps when she came to know him better she would tell him more. Until then, simply knowing her name was enough. "Then, Isolde, is there anything you need from here other than your bow and your quiver that you'd like to take back to the castle with you?"

She laughed suddenly, her face alive with amusement. "Since I did not fell a deer as I intended this morning, there is nothing."

As her warm laughter moved over him, the chill that had followed him home from the West Indies eased. "Then let us make our way to my horse before the snowfall gets heavier."

"Are you no longer used to Scottish winters after being in

the West Indies for so long?" she asked as they made their way to his horse.

This time it was his turn to laugh. "The heart of a Scotsman remains in Scotland no matter where his travels take him. While away, I dreamed of the craggy hills of the Quiraing, the open moors covered in heather blossoms, and the shores of Dunvegan at sunset. This is my home, no matter the season." Careful to avoid her injured arm, he lifted her and settled her on his horse before mounting the animal behind her. With a light flick of the reins, he signalled Phoenix to head for home.

Once they settled into a rhythm on the back of the horse, Orrick's attention shifted back to the woman in his arms. She smelled of burnt flesh, but also an intriguing combination of smoky peat and Scottish rose. Her skin was still clean despite her dishevelled state. Gazing at her profile, he couldn't shake the feeling that he'd seen her before. It bothered him that he couldn't remember where they'd met, but he would solve the puzzle. He always did.

In the short term, he had more serious matters to think about. Like how he would introduce her to his family. He'd told no one he would be returning with a mysterious woman. There was no doubt they would welcome Isolde. But with her being female, they might jump to conclusions about what connected the two of them. He was simply offering aid to a fellow warrior. That she happened to be female was not something within his control.

To avoid questions, perhaps he could whisk her inside with no one knowing, or at least until he was ready to answer to his kin. For he had a feeling there was far more to the story of her life in the cave than she was willing to share at present.

When he and Isolde passed through the gates of Dunvegan, Orrick's heart sank to see Alastair, Tormod, Gwendolyn, and Fiona waiting to receive him. So much for escorting Isolde in unnoticed. "Prepare yourself." It was all the warning he could give her before his kin came forward to greet them.

When Orrick stopped before them and dismounted, Alastair's gaze shifted from his brother to the woman he lifted off the horse and kept close by his side.

"You left in such a hurry, we were worried something had gone amiss," Alastair said, continuing to study Isolde.

"I should have said something before I raced out of here. It was Isolde who rescued Emlyn from the badger, not me. Her arm is seriously injured. She needs to see Healer Lottie as soon as possible."

Tormod frowned as he sniffed the air. "Why do you both smell like burnt flesh?"

"It's a long story." Orrick slipped his arm about Isolde's waist and propelled them towards the castle, forcing the others to follow along. Isolde flinched away from his touch, but he held firm. The sooner they got inside the fewer questions there would be.

Alastair hurried to the doorway then stopped, blocking the way inside. "I think the womenfolk can see to Isolde's needs better than you can. Why don't you stay here and inform Tormod and me on all that has happened this morning?" The determination in his brother's expression said he would not take nay for an answer.

Before Orrick could respond, Gwendolyn came forward and took Isolde's arm. "Let's leave the men to their discussion. Fiona and I would be more than happy to see to your care. Come." Gwendolyn propelled Isolde forward, across the threshold and away from him. Only the slight widening of Isolde's eyes hinted at dread. It wasn't until she was out of sight that Orrick realised he still held her quiver and bow.

"Would you care to explain how you came to be in the presence of Isolde Nicolson?" Alastair asked, the lines between his brows deepening.

"Nicolson? Is that her clan name?" Orrick frowned. "She said no clan would claim her as their own."

"Who is she?" Tormod asked, arching his brow. "In her dishevelled state, she looks more like a child of the fairies than anything human."

"She bleeds like the rest of us, though I dare say she is braver than most," Orrick said. "While searching for the lost girl, I came upon her near MacLeod's Tables, hunting red deer. During the badger attack, when I failed to strike the animal with my arrow, Isolde threw herself at the badger and child, breaking the badger's hold on Emlyn's leg. Before she could move away, the badger sank its teeth into her arm—a wound she sealed herself while I returned Emlyn to Dunvegan. I knew she was injured and I had to go back for her. Her injured state is because of my hesitation." Orrick looked away from his brothers' probing gazes. "My inability to fight almost got her killed."

Tormod made a disgusted sound. "Her injuries are not your fault, Orrick."

"Aye. They are." Orrick set his jaw as he glared at his brother. "One day when I hesitate, someone truly will die. It's only a matter of time."

"Enough of that kind of talk." Alastair's voice came out hard as he looked from Orrick to Tormod. "We have more important matters to address. The Nicolson clan is our ally. It is well known among the clans that John Nicolson banished Isolde over a year ago. If Laird Nicolson learns we are harbouring his sister, he will end his allegiance to the MacLeods. As soon as Isolde Nicolson is bandaged, we must return her to whatever hole she crept out of."

Orrick's blood raced with the heat of his anger even as he wondered why Isolde had been banished from her home. None of them had been on the Isle of Skye when whatever happened between the laird and his sister had transpired. And it wasn't like Alastair to give credence to idle gossip. "What has gotten into you, Alastair? In the past you let your own eyes make judgements. When did that change? Or is it only because I am involved in this situation and not Tormod?"

Alastair flinched at the insinuation that he favoured Tormod over Orrick. "My response has nothing to do with you and me, or the past. My burdens are heavy at the moment. We have the English on one side pressing all of us to pledge fealty to their king. On the other side, we have the MacDonalds gathering the Highland clans against us. We will soon be at war, mark my words, no matter how hard I have tried to negotiate peace."

"Aye," Orrick replied, trying to keep his anger in check. "These are trying times. We have weathered our share of storms in the past. We will find our way through this one as well by working together and by helping all those in need of our help, no matter what side of the clan divide they fall on."

Tormod shook his head. "You always were a bit idealistic, Orrick. Alastair is right about this. We need the Nicolsons to fight with us against the English and the MacDonalds."

"From what I saw in the wilderness, Isolde is more an asset than a detriment. Besides, the two of you are getting ahead of yourselves. No one outside the immediate family even knows she is here," Orrick said, digging in his heels. He would not abandon a woman who was injured because of his lack of action. "Allow Lottie to heal Isolde's arm so she can continue to protect herself with her bow and arrow. Then, we will talk about sending her away."

Alastair frowned. "You mean keep her presence here a

secret?"

Orrick shrugged. "It wouldn't be that difficult. With the state of her injuries I doubt she will be roaming the castle hallways anytime soon."

"Our brother has a point." Tormod shifted his gaze between Alastair and Orrick. "The girl hasn't been seen in these parts for more than a year. It wouldn't be that hard to keep her identity a secret."

Alastair's features steeled. "I will agree if you give the girl another name so no one can connect the sudden appearance of a female stranger with the year-ago disappearance of Laird Nicolson's sister."

"Agreed." Orrick felt the tension in his shoulders suddenly ease. "Of the three of us, I know best how to stay to the shadows. That has been my role in this family for as long as I can remember. Stay back and stay quiet while you and Tormod take care of everything." Orrick stepped around Alastair and headed for the door. This time Alastair didn't stop him.

"That is not what I meant, Orrick," Alastair objected as Orrick continued inside.

It might not be what he said, but it was how his two brothers always treated him. The three of them were all adults now. It was up to Orrick to decide how he lived his life from this moment forward. If he didn't think he could ever lift a sword against another human again, then he had to find a different way forward. Part of that new beginning would be listening to all sides of a story before he passed judgement on anyone. Even if Alastair would not, Orrick wanted to hear from Isolde's own lips what had happened between her and her brother to cause her current circumstances.

Until that time, there were other things that demanded his attention, such as making sure the woman didn't die from her wounds.

CHAPTER FIVE

I SOLDE FORCED HERSELF to breathe as she walked alongside the two MacLeod women to the upper chambers of the castle. They entered a room halfway down the hall. Once inside, the two women stared at her in a long silence. Isolde straightened and held her head high, trying not to let their exploring gazes ruffle her composure. She kept her hands at her sides and let them look their fill as she studied them in return.

The blond-haired woman's loose-fitting green damask gown was designed to hide her thickened waist and full breasts, indicating that she was with child. The red-haired woman wore a soft peach-coloured silk gown with a stomacher and petticoat embroidered in green and lavender flowers. Their hair was neatly combed and swept back from their faces in refined styles. Isolde swallowed, knowing she looked a sight compared to these elegant women.

The blonde shook her head as though breaking whatever trance she'd been in and stepped forward. "Forgive us. We are being rude." She offered Isolde a slight curtsey. "I am Gwendolyn, the laird's wife. And this is Fiona, Tormod's wife." She looked directly at Isolde. "How do you know Orrick?"

"I don't," she lied.

"How did you become injured?" Fiona asked, studying her cloak with interest.

Isolde nervously folded her hands before her. "We met this morning while he was looking for the lost child, and I was hunting."

Fiona's gaze narrowed. "That's how you got injured?"

Isolde nodded her head. "I was attacked by the same badger that chewed Emlyn's leg. Where is the child? Will she survive her injuries?"

"The girl fell asleep after Lottie put a new poultice over her wounds. She could do the same for you. Why don't you give me your cloak?"

Isolde unfastened the cloak. She slipped the bloody garment from her shoulders, exposing her singed and still-seeping arm just as footsteps sounded at the doorway.

"Why is there blood all the way up the stairs and into this chamber?" A dark-haired young woman came inside, stopping abruptly at the sight of Isolde. Alarm crossed her features. "What is she doing here? This woman is dangerous." The girl propelled herself between Isolde and Gwendolyn, forcing the laird's wife to take several steps back. "Get away from my sister-in-law. I'll not let you hurt her."

"Rowena!" Gwendolyn's face paled as she shifted to the

angry woman's side. "Isolde is a guest here. She is no threat to any of us."

"I refuse to allow her to stay under this roof." Rowena's dark eyes fairly sparked as she put her hand out, blocking Gwendolyn from advancing. "She is ruthless and attacks pregnant women without provocation."

Fiona's brow furrowed. "Why would you say such a thing?"

"She nearly killed my friend Sarah Nicolson's child with her bow and arrow."

"Sarah is alive? And her child?" Isolde asked in a tight voice.

Rowena scowled. "They live, in spite of what you did to them."

At the news, the weight of Isolde's guilt lifted from her shoulders. All this time when she didn't hear about anyone other than her brother surviving the incident at Scorrybreac, she'd assumed the worst. A deep sob of relief escaped Isolde's throat as she sank to her knees. "I was so afraid . . ."

"The child's leg was injured by your arrow. She walks, but not as other children do."

A girl. "I am so sorry," Isolde choked out. Tears scalded her eyes as the agony of that day coiled in her chest yet again. How would she ever make up for all the pain she'd caused that poor innocent girl?

"Your apology won't heal her leg," Rowena bit out. "And I'll not give you the chance to harm anyone else, especially

Gwendolyn. She has suffered plenty already."

"Enough." Gwendolyn forced her way past Rowena's extended arms and made her way to Isolde's side. She knelt beside Isolde and placed a hand upon her shoulder. "There are always two sides to every story." She pointed to Isolde's damaged arm and dishevelled state. "Isolde certainly hasn't come away unscathed by whatever happened."

Gwendolyn lifted her gaze to Rowena. "Give her a chance to explain once she is returned to health herself. Judging by the blood on her cloak, I'd say she's greatly in need of our help and compassion."

"I'll go get Lottie," Fiona said, exiting the chamber.

"Would you go to the kitchen and ask for water to clean her wounds, Rowena?"

Rowena hesitated then nodded. At the doorway she added, "It will take more than water to clean away what spoils this one's soul." Then she was gone.

"Pay Rowena no mind." Gwendolyn put an arm around Isolde's waist and helped her stand. "Rowena has become overly protective of all of us during the past few months. She doesn't mean what she says."

"If she does, I would not blame her," Isolde said, leaning on Gwendolyn as they made their way towards the bed.

Gwendolyn settled her atop the coverlet and sat beside her. "I am convinced there is more to the story than what Rowena has heard from her friend."

"There is, but that doesn't change anything that happened." All of Isolde's strength suddenly vanished. She shivered as a chill came over her body and a numbness entered her soul. She closed her eyes and wished for the millionth time that her brother would someday forgive her for what happened, and that she could somehow escape being forced back into spying on her countrymen if she were ever discovered by the English. Even death would be a welcome release from that form of conscription again.

"Isolde." Gwendolyn's voice reached out to her, pulling her back from sleep. "Stay with me until Lottie tends to your arm."

"Are you not afraid of me after what Rowena said?" Isolde forced the words past her suddenly dry throat. "Perhaps I am as horrible as she fears."

Gwendolyn smiled. "All men and women wear masks to protect themselves, Isolde. Your cloak was your mask. You willingly took it off when asked." Gwendolyn shrugged. "That, if nothing else, tells me what lies in your heart. Once you stay here for a time, the others will take off their masks as well."

Did Isolde care what lay in the hearts of those around her? She wasn't planning to stay long at Dunvegan. Only until she healed enough to protect herself once more.

Any further conversation died as the door opened and a man entered the chamber, carrying a bowl and a pitcher of steaming water, which he set by the bed on a table.

After the man departed, Rowena entered bearing a tray

of food. She was accompanied by an older woman. In her hands, the woman carried a large bag that she set beside the water. Following the two women was Orrick.

He strode towards the bed and stood beside Gwendolyn. "I can stay with her now."

Gwendolyn stood, then stepped away. Orrick immediately slipped into her place and offered Isolde a soft smile. She was drawn by the sheer intensity of his manner. His dark eyes were upon her, brilliant, sparkling with vitality in his handsome face.

"That is quite a wound you have there, my dear," the healer said in a soothing voice. "'Twas very brave of you to staunch the bleeding yourself." She sat on the bed opposite Orrick and studied Isolde's blackened marks on her upper arm. "You did an admirable job, considering how painful that must have been." She opened her bag and withdrew a small brown vial. She removed the stopper and handed it to Isolde. "Drink this. It will help with the pain and make my job a little easier on us both."

Orrick nodded. "Lottie knows what she is doing. I will remain beside you the whole time."

After releasing a pent-up breath, Isolde did as instructed and drank the entire contents of the vial before handing it back to the healer.

"Very good," Lottie stated. "Let's clean out that wound so that I might stitch what you failed to seal."

Instead of tensing as Lottie peeled back fragments of

charred skin from Isolde's arm, the medicine Lottie had given Isolde helped her relax into the softness of the bed.

Orrick brought his hand to rest over Isolde's. "You're going to be well enough. Lottie will take care of you. Rest while she works. It will be the best thing for you." Following a light squeeze, he pulled his hand away.

She suddenly felt terribly alone without Orrick's reassuring touch. She wanted to take his hand again and hold on to him. Strange. She couldn't remember the last time she had accepted solace from anyone.

"Not many men would have borne such pain as you did sealing that wound," Orrick said in a soft voice.

A faint smile touched Isolde's lips as she closed her eyes. "Women are forced to tolerate pain far above that which men could endure on a regular basis."

A soft, male chuckle sounded as she slid further into a relaxed state. "How right you are, warrior girl. How right you are."

ISOLDE AWAKENED IN the middle of the night to find herself tucked beneath the covers of a strange bed. The golden glow of flames from a recently banked fire glowed in the hearth. She sat up, trying to put the bits and pieces darting through her mind back together. When her gaze drifted to a chair beside the bed, and the sleeping warrior in it, she remembered everything.

She had been injured and Orrick MacLeod had taken her back to Dunvegan. Every moment she spent here brought danger to the entire clan. Some of those she'd met yesterday understood that—Rowena, Alastair, and Tormod. Yet others had put that threat behind them to care for her—Orrick, Gwendolyn, and Fiona. Their acceptance of her, despite the risks, warmed her heart, knowing there was still kindness in a world that had shown her little in the past few years since her parents died.

Even so, she could not stay with the MacLeods long. She would not repay their kindness with suffering. Her gaze travelled over the face of the man at her bedside. His features at rest appeared softer. His face was less angular, his cheeks less sculpted, his lips less firm. It was as though in sleep he could be himself and not what others expected him to be. Isolde knew that sentiment all too well.

His lids flickered, then opened to reveal those dark eyes that always saw too much. "You were very restless during the night."

She stiffened, then forced herself to relax. "I am not used to a soft bed, the warmth of the fire, or company."

"If you would prefer less comfortable accommodations—"

"I did not mean—" She bit her lower lip. "I am grateful for all you've done to help me."

He sat forward in his chair. His gaze searched her face. "How are you feeling? Lottie said you might run a fever."

"I am better. I should probably go. Even though I was injured and not quite myself yesterday, I could tell I was the cause of much friction between you and your brothers." She pushed the covers off, intending to get up when she saw she was dressed not in her rags but a soft linen night rail that was so thin and sheer it was almost transparent. She pulled the covers back.

"My brothers are not heartless. They have agreed to protect you while you recover, Isolde Nicolson."

Her heart stumbled. "You know who I am?" *And what I've done?*

"My brothers seemed to recognise you immediately. You looked familiar to me when we met, but I still cannot recall where we met before. You wouldn't care to enlighten me?"

Isolde dropped her gaze to the coverlet. Once she told him, the judgement that filled the eyes of others would also be reflected in his brown eyes. She issued a soft sigh. It was inevitable he would find out. Best if it came from her lips. "We met at the Highland games six summers ago. You were there with your friends when you came upon me preparing for the archery tournament." She returned her gaze to his. "You mocked me for being a female archer."

His brows furrowed, as if searching his memories. Then the lines between his brows smoothed and he smiled. "That was you?" He chuckled. "Well, we might have laughed at you, but you put us all in our places when you won the tournament."

She didn't share his amusement. "I've spent my life proving that I am a skilled archer and worthy of fighting alongside men. I am as hard and calculating as any male warrior."

He sobered. "I apologise that I was amongst those who belittled your skill." He gazed at her without speaking for a moment. "I think you are not as hard as you'd like others to believe. You were quite concerned for the safety of the little girl when the badger attacked."

"I acted on impulse and was punished for it. Don't make the mistake of thinking I am soft and feminine."

He smiled. "You don't believe feminine attributes have any place in a warrior's life?"

"Not if she wants to survive in a world of men."

His smile increased. "Wait until you get to know Gwendolyn, Fiona, and Rowena better before you make that judgement part of who you are. They are three of the most feminine yet fearsome women I know. But that will happen only if you stay here a while. It is my intent to stay by your bedside until you and I can start strengthening your arm once more."

Isolde set her jaw stubbornly. "Go to your own bed. I have no need of you."

"You did me a favour by saving Emlyn. Therefore I must do a service for you in return. I'll stay with you until you are able to care for yourself again."

"I am able to care for myself now."

His brows arched. "If that is so, then stand and walk to the door."

Isolde pressed her lips together and pushed back the covers once again. What did it matter if he could see through her gown? For once she made it to the door, she would never see him again. She put her feet on the floor and stood. The room swayed before her eyes. She bit down on her lip, determined to take a step, and her knees buckled.

If Orrick hadn't bolted from his chair to catch her, she would have fallen to the floor. He carefully returned her to the bed. "Is that enough evidence for you that you are not quite ready to leave this place?" He pulled the covers over her. "Let us take care of you."

An odd sensation moved through her chest at how gentle he was with her. No man had ever treated her in such a way. "You'll soon regret asking me to stay. I am not a good patient. I detest being ill."

"And I detest bad-tempered patients. I will be as bad-natured as you so that you will get well quickly just to be rid of me."

A reluctant smile came to her lips. "Stay if you like. Who am I to refuse your hospitality?"

"I'm glad you came to your senses. In the meanwhile, while you are here, Alastair has asked that we call you something other than Isolde for the staff's sake and in an effort to keep your identity a secret. Is there another name you would like to be called?"

She felt an odd pang but forced it aside. He had every reason to ask. "My mother used to call me Izzy. Is that different enough?"

"For the staff, aye."

She didn't want to ask, but she would never be able to relax unless she did, so she forced herself to form the words. "If you know who I am, do you also know why I was out in the wilderness?"

He shook his head. "I will let you tell me that story when you are ready."

She released a pent-up breath. She wasn't strong enough to tell him right now. She needed her strength to be able to guard herself, her emotions. Because once she told him the truth, he would turn on her the way Rowena had. Rowena knew a partial truth, being friends with Sarah, but not the whole truth.

Would Orrick's sister tell him her version of the tale? It was a risk Isolde would have to take until she felt stronger, more able to put up her defences. She closed her eyes against his probing gaze and sank back against the bed. "I'll tell you later."

"I can wait until then," Orrick replied in a clear and even tone. "We all have secrets. Who am I to judge you when I have so many of my own?" He placed his hand over hers where it rested atop the coverlet.

Though she tried to stop herself, she found her fingers turning and curling against the warmth and comfort he offered. Her eyes remained closed but she felt her lips pull up in a smile at the thought that Orrick MacLeod had secrets. Would he ever tell her any of his secrets? Were any of them as hard to live with as her own?

———————

FROM HER PERCH near Dunvegan Castle, Aria concealed her unusual white hair with her cloak and hid amongst the shadows as she had done most of her life. Over the past two weeks, since she'd come forth into the human realm, she'd learned that Norman MacLeod was dead. That the man had died a painful death from some unknown disease brought her no comfort. Instead, she was filled with a loss of purpose. The last thirteen years of her life had been focused on revenge against one certain man who no longer existed.

If she couldn't have revenge, then perhaps she could have answers. The man's children might be able to help her understand why he had refused her. Or would they refuse her as well? So far from her observations she'd learned very little about those who now led the MacLeod clan.

Watching the MacLeods and listening to their conversations, she'd learned that Alastair MacLeod was the new heir. The clan had conflicts with both the MacQueens and the MacDonalds. And that one of the brothers, Orrick, had discovered an intriguing woman in the wilderness. That woman had been taken into the MacLeods' home despite her peculiar nature. Back home, Aria was a bow-woman herself.

Aria smiled into the darkness. The woman in pelts was dangerous, but then so was Aria. Perhaps the MacLeods wouldn't dismiss her because she was a warrior woman. Judging by the other women she had observed, the new male residents of the castle seemed to like strong women as their companions. Perhaps she should stop hiding and simply walk up to the gates and introduce herself. Aria straightened, ready to take that first step when self-doubt swamped her.

Were humans as vicious as the fairies towards creatures who were different? Would they refuse her? Mock her? Threaten to imprison her as their father had tried to do?

Aria stepped back into the shadows. She didn't have enough information yet to take such a risk. Until she did, she had to keep herself hidden.

She'd had a chance in Fairyland to be with another human—the male child her grandfather had stolen from the MacLeods. But Aria wanted nothing to do with marrying the human male the king had chosen for her. Though magic had been used on him to age him until he had reached Aria's own age in human years of twenty, he was more like a brother to her than a potential mate. Such a union would never take place if Aria had any say in the matter.

At that moment a thought occurred to her. Perhaps instead of seeking revenge against the MacLeods, she could help them recover their missing brother. How could they refuse her if she offered to restore their own human family?

But again, it would take time to plan how to make that a reality. Oberon wouldn't let the male he had taken as his own son leave without a fight.

She needed to think about how to present such an offer to the MacLeods so that they got something they wanted and she would get the family she wanted in return. A sense of purpose flooded her. For the first time in many years hope blossomed inside Aria's chest as her need for revenge fell away, replaced by a new goal: a family who would accept her for who she was. It was all she'd ever wanted.

CHAPTER SIX

I SOLDE'S TEMPERATURE BEGAN to rise, and rise again, later that morning. Orrick stood at the back of the chamber while Lottie bathed her patient's head with cool water. That was, until a scream tore through the chamber. In her fevered state, Isolde arched off the bed, spilling the basin of water beside her. Her eyes were still closed as she swung her arms and jerked as though trying to get away from some unseen foe.

Orrick rushed forward and grabbed Isolde's arms. "Is this normal?"

Lottie gave him a sad smile. "Unfortunately, aye, when a fever runs high."

Orrick struggled to hold down one arm and then the other. The minute he got her arms settled she lashed out again. "Do you have anything I can use to restrain her?"

Lottie hurried to the bureau and came back with a handful of ribbons. "These used to be your mother's ribbons. They are the best I can do unless I go belowstairs."

"The ribbons are perfect." He took three of them and awkwardly plaited them together while still trying to hold

Isolde in place on the bed. When that restraint was complete, he released Isolde momentarily and tied the ribbon to the bedpost before reaching for her hand, but she struggled so violently she spilled out of the bed and onto the floor.

Lottie gasped and moved to Isolde's side.

She did not awaken when she hit the cold, wooden surface. Instead, she calmed momentarily. "Leave her there while I get this other restraint prepared." Orrick plaited the ribbons and secured them to the opposite bedpost in record time. Once finished, he bent beside Isolde, scooped her up into his arms, and settled her once more on the bed.

He took advantage of her stillness to tie her left wrist to one bedpost and her right wrist to the other.

"Nay. Nay. Stay away!" Isolde's scream made them both jump.

"The poor lamb," Lottie said, moving to wipe the water from the floor. "The miss's dreams sound more like terrors."

"Isolde," Orrick whispered softly. He touched her arm, watching her twist and turn, jerking as if trying to get away from something. Sweat glistened on her skin and strands of her blond hair stuck to her face and neck.

"Let me go, Lieutenant!" Her whole body was shaking.

This time, Orrick cupped her face in his hands, gently. "You're safe, Isolde. No one here will harm you."

Her eyes opened, and in them Orrick saw terror and hopeless, excruciating fear. Then the fear was gone. Her body sagged, the shaking gone. "I was dreaming."

"Aye," he said softly, stroking her wet cheeks. "The dream is over. You are safe with me."

She stared up into his face and offered a weak smile. A heartbeat later her smile became a frown as she turned her head towards the bedpost on her left, forcing his hands to slip away. "Why am I tied to the bed?" There was a touch of panic in her voice.

He quickly released her. "It was necessary to keep you from hurting yourself. You fell onto the floor once."

She massaged her wrists as she tried to sit up, but a shudder went through her. "I am not used to . . . this kind . . . of bed." Her teeth were clenched to keep them from chattering. "Might I have . . . another blanket?" she asked as chills racked her.

"I will have to go find one," Lottie said before turning to go.

Before he could think of a reason not to, Orrick pulled the covers back and slipped into bed beside her. He pulled her back against his front, spooning her. He felt her stiffen. "I am not going to hurt you. I am only warming you until Lottie returns." As the warmth of his body moved into her, her shuddering lessened, then stopped. "You should try to rest. Sleep will heal you faster than anything else."

"What if I dream again?"

"I'll be here to wake you." A few minutes later he felt her relax, her breathing deepen.

While she slept, Orrick felt his own muscles tense as he

pondered who the lieutenant she spoke of in her dreams could be. A sudden need to find the bastard who'd hurt Isolde consumed him. He'd find out who it was . . . and then what? He'd given up his sword. Or would finding the bastard and looking him in the eye be enough to encourage Orrick to pick up his weapon once more?

<center>~~~</center>

"ORRICK?" HER VOICE broke through the silence on the evening of the second day.

"Shh. I'm here." From the chair beside the bed, he smoothed her hair back from her cheeks, running his fingers along her clammy skin. He heard a whimper from her throat and he moved to sit beside her, pulling her into his arms. She nestled against his chest, and old memories came flooding back to Orrick. Memories of holding his fellow soldiers in his arms while they drew their last breath, rocking their war-ravaged bodies until their life seeped from them. They needed his comfort then as Isolde needed him now.

But this was different. Isolde was not dying. She simply needed him until her fever broke, demanding nothing in return. The loneliness he'd brought back to Dunvegan with him eased as a warm, soft feeling coursed through him.

Lottie entered the chamber a while later, carrying a basin of water, which she set by the bedside. "Your family is gathering for dinner. I can take over here if you'd like to join them."

"Nay," Orrick said, curling his arms tightly around Isolde. "If it's all right with you, I'll stay."

Lottie nodded. "She seems calmer when you are near."

He felt calmer when she was near him as well. At the sound of their voices, Isolde stirred, then opened her eyes.

ISOLDE'S HEAD THROBBED—A low, dull ache at her temples. Her mouth was dry, and she felt a hollowness at the centre of her being. She once again tried to place where she was, surrounded by warmth and comfort—two things she'd had little of over the past year. Her memory returned more swiftly this time as she realised Orrick held her in his arms. She'd awakened several times over the past many hours to find him right there beside her.

Lottie was by the bedside as well, watching Isolde with a concerned expression. "How are you feeling?"

"Better, I suppose, but thirsty."

"That is good to hear." Relief coloured the healer's tone.

Orrick sat up to hold a mug before her. "You gave us quite a scare."

She accepted the mug and brought the cool liquid to her lips, drinking slowly. When she was done, she handed the mug back to him, and pulled back, out of his arms. He shifted off the bed, returning to the chair. It was then she noticed how tired he looked.

"How long have I been asleep?"

"Two days."

"You've been here the whole time?"

He shrugged. "One of us had to stay with you. Besides, I promised I would."

"I did not mean to cause you any trouble."

He smiled.

The soft warmth of his gaze spiralled through her, warming her in a way that had nothing to do with a fever.

"Do you remember anything from the past two days?"

"Some of it." She couldn't keep the chagrin she felt from showing on her face as she massaged her wrists. "If I was violent, I apologise."

"You were deep in the throes of a fever. It was your nightmares that concerned me more than your thrashing."

Her eyes widened. "Did I cry out?"

"Who is the lieutenant?"

She groaned, burying her face in her hands and wishing this was all a bad dream.

Lottie stood. "I'll leave the two of you to talk," she said and stepped through the door, closing it softly behind her.

"Can you tell me what happened? Why you were adamant that some lieutenant stay away from you?"

The lieutenant was in her past. If she were careful, she would never have to see him again. Just as important was keeping the English officer from harming anyone else she cared for. Lieutenant Collins would punish Orrick, and the other MacLeods, if he discovered her at Dunvegan. Was she morally obligated to tell Orrick and the rest of his kin of that danger? What her brother would do to them if he learned she was there was nothing compared to what the English army would do.

She would tell him just enough to warn him. "The English took me captive." She forced the words past her dry lips.

He frowned. "I am sure there is more to the story than that."

"There is, but I'm not ready to tell all of it yet."

He nodded, remaining silent, waiting for her to say more.

"The English are trying to determine who amongst us supports the return of Charles Edward Stuart to the throne of Scotland or if we support the English king and will pledge our allegiance to him."

"How did they intend for you to discern that information? By using your skill with a bow and arrow?"

"That I would not have minded." She felt heat rise to her cheeks. "They trained me as a spy."

He sat very still, but she could see the anger dancing in the depths of his dark eyes. "That is a dangerous game."

Shame dropped into her stomach. "I quickly discovered that."

His mouth tightened and his eyes blazed. "How long were you held captive? Did these men abuse you? How long were you forced to spy? Was anyone nearby to support you?"

She stiffened. This interrogation was not what she'd intended. She shifted away, trying to push back the uncontrollable panic his words sent rushing over her. She held up her hand, cutting off the questions, and floundered for words that would satisfy him. There were some things it was better if he never knew. "I am not ready to talk about all of what happened. It was difficult, but I found a way to survive. And, as soon as I was able, to escape. That's why I was in the wilderness. I could not go back to my brother, or anywhere else. Now, your clan is in danger for harbouring me."

"The MacLeods can defend themselves—or at least most of them can." He gave a short, bitter laugh. "The English are gone for now. You have time to heal, and only then will we find a way forward."

"I was fine on my own in the wilderness." Her voice shook, and she tried desperately to control it.

"You cannot live that way forever." Orrick's gaze bored into hers.

Her heart raced in her chest. This whole conversation left her feeling off balance. "I could have." *Until I met you.*

CHAPTER SEVEN

A KNOCK CAME at the door the next morning. Isolde had hoped it would be Orrick returning after he'd left her last night. Instead, Gwendolyn opened the door. "Are you fit for a visitor or two?"

"Aye," Isolde replied from where she stood at the window with a blanket wrapped about her shoulders. Her fever had passed and she was feeling much stronger this morning. Her injury was healing well and already she could fully extend her arm. But could she hold her bow? That was a question she longed to discover; that is, if she could figure out what had happened to her weapon.

Gwendolyn slipped through the doorway, along with a small girl. Isolde moved to kneel before the child. "Emlyn, how are you?"

The girl pulled up the skirt of her dress and showed the bandages beneath. "Lottie says I can walk around the castle but not to run yet." She dropped her skirt and hung her head.

Gwendolyn scooted the little girl forward with her hands. "Emlyn would like to visit for a while. I'll be nearby should you need me."

Isolde tried to object. What did she know about children? But Gwendolyn vanished before Isolde could demand she stay. The minute the door closed all the uncertainties that had haunted her for the past fourteen months came back to her. She didn't know anything about children. She'd always been too busy training to pay much attention. Her brother's child would be toddling around by now—now that she had survived the ordeal Isolde had caused her. Or would she? Rowena had mentioned the child was lame. Had her arrow somehow deformed the child's leg?

Emlyn must have read something in Isolde's expression because she held out her hand. "Please, don't leave me alone like everyone else."

The fear inside Isolde shattered at the soft plea. She reached for the small hand. Confidently, Emlyn placed her hand in Isolde's larger one. "Let's sit on the bed, shall we?" Shortening her stride to accommodate the child's smaller legs, Isolde led her to the bedside to help her sit at the edge while she settled beside her. The little girl had been at Dunvegan for the same four days as Isolde now. She appeared healthy, with rosy cheeks and clear eyes. Yet a sadness lingered behind it all.

"Emlyn, do you remember anything about what happened in the wilderness?"

The little girl shuddered, as if remembering everything she had endured. "Those men came to the village. They attacked everyone and set fire to the houses. That's when I ran into the woods and kept running. I was still running when the badger attacked."

A surge of protectiveness welled up in Isolde and she reached up to stroke a wisp of the child's blond hair away from her wide, frightened eyes. Isolde startled when the little girl thrust herself against Isolde's chest and nestled into her body. Tears welled in Emlyn's eyes and spilled down her cheeks. Acting on instinct, Isolde curled her good arm around Emlyn in an embrace as her own mother had done when she was a child. She rocked back and forth, not knowing what else to do or say. The motion seemed to calm Emlyn, because she stopped crying.

A slow warmth curled inside Isolde's stomach, and the hollowness she'd felt for the past year seemed to vanish. She stared down at the blond head against her chest. Her heart wrenched at the sight. Emlyn had needed comfort, yet it was Isolde who felt her muscles relax and her own anxiety lessen. Who would have thought she was capable of giving comfort, and feeling content in return? Was this what motherhood would feel like?

The memory of Orrick's lean muscular body pressed close to hers during her fever filled Isolde's thoughts. He had proven himself to be kind and compassionate over the past few days, unlike so many of the men she had known all her life. He would make the perfect mate . . .

Isolde stiffened. She had no right to think such thoughts

of Orrick or any man. She'd made her choice long ago to be only a warrior, never a wife or a mother, and that had led her to her current circumstances. It was madness to even consider things that would only hinder her goal.

Emlyn sniffled, then sat back, staring up at Isolde, her gaze filled with innocence. "Will you teach me?"

"Teach you what?"

Emlyn jumped down from the bed, her memories of the tragedy she'd suffered now gone. She stood before Isolde with her chin up and her spine straight. "I want you to teach me how to be brave and strong like you."

Isolde didn't know what to say. No one, male or female, had ever said such a thing to her before. "I can teach you how to protect yourself."

"I want to use a bow and arrow like you."

Isolde frowned. "If you still feel that way when you are older, I would be honoured to teach you." If she were still alive by then. The sombre thought came into Isolde's mind before she could stop it.

Emlyn's lip came out in a pout. "That will take forever."

"Not as long as you think." Isolde ruffled the little girl's hair, then jerked her hand away, surprised she could do something so spontaneous. "Perhaps later this week we can both work on strengthening exercises if you'd like?"

With a nod of the little girl's head, doubts assailed Isolde. She frowned. What had possessed her to make such an offer? She had no right to move about this castle as she pleased. She had no right to stay any longer than was necessary. And what would happen to Emlyn when she did leave? For she couldn't take the child with her and condemn her to a life of total isolation.

Isolde clamped her hands before her to keep them from shaking. She would have no choice but to do to Emlyn what everyone else in her life had done to her: leave.

Isolde's thoughts were disrupted by the clatter of hoof-beats outside at the front of the castle. She sprang to her feet and moved to the window. Judging by the sound, there were multiple horses arriving at Dunvegan over the drawbridge. She pushed aside the shutters and peered below. Her heart stuttered in her chest at the sight of familiar red jackets. The English had arrived. The sight sent terror spinning through Isolde.

She studied the twenty men on horses advancing into the courtyard below. Surely they were not here to do battle, for there were far more MacLeods who could fight and over-whelm the small contingent of soldiers. Nay, they were here for another purpose. To find her? To threaten the MacLeods as they had other clans on the isle?

That was when one man separated himself from the oth-ers to ride at the head of the group. Lieutenant Collins. He came to a stop in front of the group of fifty MacLeods who had assembled outside and dismounted. Instead of approach-ing Alastair, Collins stopped and looked up, directly at the window from which she peered down.

Isolde shrank back out of sight as her heart pounded in her ears. She was up at least two storeys in the castle, with no light behind her. It would be impossible, if the lieutenant had truly seen her, to fully identify her. Isolde clenched her fingers, longing to hold her bow and quiver. At least with her weapon in hand, she might be able to defend herself. "Emlyn. Go find Gwendolyn and stay with her."

"What's wrong?" the child asked, her eyes wide and frightened once more.

"Please. It is urgent that you do what I say."

The little girl nodded and left the chamber.

Isolde fought the urge to run. If the English found her leaving Dunvegan, she would only make things worse for the MacLeods. But she wasn't about to stay in her chamber either.

Retrieving the discarded ribbons near the bedside, Isolde used them to fashion her blanket into a makeshift gown over her sleeping shift. Once that was complete, she headed for the door. It was imperative she find where Orrick and the others had stored her weapon. That, or find some other weapon with which to defend herself and the others in this castle. The MacLeods had taken the girl out of the wilderness, but no one could take the warrior out of this girl.

DISTANT BUT STEADILY advancing hoofbeats came towards

the castle's courtyard. Orrick's hands slowly clenched into fists as he watched the English soldiers. One man broke away from the columns of men to position his horse at the front.

Alastair, Tormod, Orrick, and Graeme Duff, the Dunvegan captain of the guard, all stood together with their swords at their sides while fifty of the castle guards settled behind them, ready to fight should that become necessary.

"I thought the English had retreated for the winter?" Tormod asked of no one in particular.

"Follow my lead," Alastair said. "Try to act as though everything is normal at this castle. Let me do the talking and see if we can end this with a dialogue. If things get out of hand, watch Graeme for the signal to attack."

Tormod rose up on the balls of his feet and fisted then relaxed his hands as excitement crossed his features. Orrick had seen that look of exhilaration on his brother's face many times in the West Indies. No matter the odds or what was at stake, Tormod loved the thrill of battle. And Alastair, he would try diplomacy every time before resorting to the sword.

In the past, Orrick might have played the part of the deceiver and battled the English in a different way. Yet, until he vanquished this thing inside him—the memories of those lives he'd taken—he would avoid battle if at all possible.

"Hold steady," Graeme said, his gaze intense as the leader of the English troops dismounted and came forward. The man in the scarlet jacket paused and looked up for a moment before returning his gaze to those before him and offering them a rigid bow. "Lieutenant Cornelius Collins of the twenty-ninth regiment."

"Why are you here?" Alastair asked bluntly without introducing himself.

Collins's eyes were small and ferret-like, and they flicked over the men standing before him as though trying to discern their secrets. "The commander-in-chief of Scotland asked me to return to follow up on reports of clan unrest. Word has reached us that clan MacQueen raided the village of Orbost five days ago. We passed by on our way here. There doesn't seem to be much left of the village or anyone who lived there."

"We brought those who survived back to Dunvegan where we can protect them," Alastair said.

The lieutenant's eyes narrowed to slits. "Protect them from your own people? Is this what the Highlands have become? Herders and fishermen attacking their own mothers for sport?" The lieutenant laughed and the men behind him shared a laugh as well. "I've heard rumours that the MacLeods are the Guardians of the Isles. What will you do, MacLeod? Shelter everyone in this godforsaken land behind your castle walls?"

"If I must." Alastair's voice was a sheet of ice and Orrick knew his brother having a difficult time finding a diplomatic tone in the face of such accusations.

Orrick watched as the lieutenant's hand moved towards

the pistol in his belt. With a forced laugh, Orrick shifted towards the man and clapped an arm around his shoulders, stopping the lieutenant's movements. "Where are our manners? We should invite you in for a wee dram and talk about this like civilised men. What say you, brothers?" *Deflection. It was one of his tricks.* Orrick knew it had worked when he felt the lieutenant's shoulders relax.

"Do you distil the whisky yourselves?" Lieutenant Collins asked with interest, allowing Orrick to lead him inside.

"We have a small distillery set up on the isle that uses peated malt and grain from Speyside and the Highlands." Alastair stared at Orrick as though he'd gone daft. Orrick knew what he was doing, bringing the Englishman inside. They'd share some spirits like gentlemen, make polite conversation, then they would send the man and his army on their way. It was the only way to make the MacLeods appear to cooperate with the English and prove they had nothing to hide.

Lieutenant Collins nodded. "I daresay Scottish whisky has been one of the better parts of being dispatched to this country."

Alastair, Tormod, and Graeme followed behind as Orrick led the Englishman to the great hall. When they entered, Becks, their steward, greeted them. "I heard your conversation below and I've set the head table with all that you desire." Indeed, six bottles of MacLeod whisky and several glasses had been set out for their use.

Only the lieutenant and six of his men sat. The others stood along the walls, watching those seated around the table. Orrick tensed when he heard a startled intake of breath. He traced the sound to a lump of tartan under a table at the back of the room. With luck, these men would be so focused on what was happening at the table that they wouldn't notice anything out of the ordinary. Acting as though they had meetings such as this every day, Becks opened two of the bottles and poured a generous splash into the glasses before placing them in front of the Englishmen.

Lieutenant Collins was the first to raise his glass and take a sip of the amber liquid. He finished with a smile. "Perfection."

"Why did you come back to Scotland?" Alastair asked from his seat across from the lieutenant. "I doubt it was concern for the villagers of Orbost."

Lieutenant Collins took another sip before answering. "Lieutenant General Handasyd was concerned that the Highlanders were going to war."

"That's a very real possibility," Orrick said flatly. "But I also think the English government knows that my brother, Alastair, is the last nail into that powder keg. Alastair is a man of peace—a diplomat. Determined not to fight unless there is no other alternative."

Lieutenant Collins peered over the brim of his glass. "With his fellow Scots or the English?"

"An English invasion would unite the isle and Highland

clans faster than if Prince Charlie returned," Tormod said without looking up from his glass.

"Is that what you support? The return of the Pretender?" The reply was shot back, stiff with indignation.

Tormod sat back and stared at their guest, his eyes alight with challenge. "I said nothing of the sort. Merely stating a fact that I think you *Sassenach* forget sometimes while you patrol the isle. Your presence only makes the Scots want to sharpen their *clai'mors.*"

"Tormod, this is supposed to be a civil dialogue," Alastair said, warning his brother to end the antagonistic conversation now before things became heated.

Lieutenant Collins set his empty glass down and peered at both Alastair and Tormod through narrowed eyes. "If you want to guarantee safety for your family, you could always declare your fealty to the king. When the English armies come—and they will come, I promise you—such an alliance might spare your loved ones."

Alastair stood. "At this particular point in time, I believe in leaving alliances the way they are. My loyalty will always be to the isle and her people."

"I admire your commitment to your people, but that could soon turn to stupidity if you are not careful." Lieutenant Collins's voice was as cold as steel as he and his men stood. The lieutenant grabbed a capped bottle of whisky off the table and with angry footsteps headed for the door. Alastair, Tormod, and Graeme followed, leaving Orrick and one other occupant in the chamber.

As the footsteps retreated, Orrick moved to the back of the room. The tension in his shoulders relaxed for the first time since they'd entered the chamber with the Englishmen. "What were you thinking, being out of your bedchamber?"

The woman beneath the tartan cloth unfurled and crawled out from under the table until she stood before Orrick. "I was searching for my bow and quiver when you and those men entered. What was I to do? Announce myself to the lieutenant?"

The lieutenant? "Lieutenant Collins was the man you talked about in your fevered dreams? He was the man from your nightmares?"

Her pale face was all the answer he needed.

"If he'd seen you . . ."

"That's why I need my weapon back. Please? It is more urgent now than ever."

He wanted to ask her what she meant, but he was suddenly distracted by her clothing. She had fashioned a sort of gown out of the tartan blanket and the ribbons he'd used to bind her during her fever. The 'dress' left her shoulders exposed and only came to her midcalf, leaving her shapely ankles bare. At the sight, warmth flooded him. Then heat, fiery heat. The woman before him was soft and feminine, yet strong and powerful. A heady combination.

Her hair was still a snarled mess, and yet the sight of her brought an unusual curl of warmth to his chest. "I'll strike a bargain with you. You let Gwendolyn help you tame your hair, and find you a more acceptable gown. This evening you'll come down to the great hall to dine with my family. Then on the morrow I will return your weapon."

Isolde glanced down at her would-be gown. "The whole idea of dining with others is rather intimidating after a year of being in a less than civilised situation."

"But you'll do it if it means reclaiming your weapon."

She swallowed roughly as she brought her gaze to his. "How can I refuse?"

He smiled, pleased that she had agreed. "Let me escort you back to your chamber. And since we are heading that way, allow me to show you one of our most prized possessions."

"The Fairy Flag?" she asked, suddenly breathless. "I've heard stories over the years of the gift given to you by the fairies."

"It was given to us by one particular fairy who was granted permission by her father, the fairy king, to marry Iain Cair MacLeod for a year and a day before being called back to Fairyland," Orrick explained as they walked from the great hall and up the stairs to the bedchambers. He stopped at the doorway of the drawing room and waved Isolde inside.

She approached the Fairy Flag with cautious steps until she stopped before where it hung between the seaward-facing windows. "It's more damaged than I expected."

"It is from the fourth century," he said from beside her.

"That is why Alastair had it preserved between two panes of glass as you see it now. He hopes to safeguard the flag for the generations who follow us."

Isolde stared at the faded yellow silk embroidered with red elf dots and crosses. "I remember the tale of how the baby's mother came back from Fairyland one night when her child was crying. She wrapped him in the silken cloth and sang him a lullaby. The details of the flag's magic are less clear in my memory."

"The legend claims the flag can be used in a time of great need to call forth the fairy legions for assistance."

Her gaze shifted from the flag to him. "The MacLeods have used it before, if I remember correctly."

"Twice, out of three chances. There is only one more use left before the flag and the flagbearer will be drawn back to Fairyland."

She gazed back at the flag. "Will Alastair use the flag if necessary?"

"I doubt it very much. He intends for the four MacLeod brothers to keep our clan safe without using the magic of the Fairy Flag." Orrick sobered at the thought that only two of the four MacLeods were capable of defending their clan should the need arise.

Callum still needed to practise his skills, and Orrick could no longer fight. Perhaps Alastair would be better served to use the flag's magic if the need arose, so at least there would be a clan to carry on those future generations.

CHAPTER EIGHT

ORRICK WAITED AT the entrance of the great hall for Isolde to appear. Gwendolyn had told him that Isolde would meet him there. The others were already inside, waiting for the two of them to join them before Mrs Morgan, their cook, and her staff brought the meal up from the kitchen. Orrick paced back and forth before the doorway, then forced himself to stop. What was wrong with him?

Was he nervous about seeing Isolde or about how his family might react to her presence at supper? Rowena and Alastair had made it quite clear that they did not want Isolde at Dunvegan. Gwendolyn's brother and sister, Samuel and Arabella, and Callum, Orrick's younger brother, had yet to meet Isolde. Would they support him in his effort to keep her safe or take Alastair's opinion as their own as they always did?

"Orrick?"

He turned at the sound of Isolde's voice, and froze. His heart stuttered in his chest and his throat constricted. She stood a few feet from him—but it was an Isolde he'd never seen before. She was dressed in a blue gown that looked like it had been made for her even though it was one of his sister's cast-offs. The dress clung to Isolde's delicate curves provocatively. Her bare shoulders and undamaged arm revealed her slim, but muscular physique. Strength and softness.

A muslin bandage covered her upper arm, but it did little to detract from the overall effect. Her hair had been washed and the chaos tamed until it shone like wheat-coloured gold that framed her delicate face. "You—you are lovely," Orrick stammered.

Isolde blushed, the heightened colour only enhancing her beauty. She nervously dropped her gaze to the floor and took a deep breath. "Gwendolyn and Fiona worked tirelessly on my hair to remove the tangles. They lathered it in sea kelp, salt, rose, and blackcurrant oil then painstakingly combed it out." She offered a demure smile. "I can still smell the blackcurrants."

Orrick stepped forward, offering her his arm and caught the faint scent, drawing it into himself. Blackcurrants and roses. He swallowed. His whole body felt hot. "When I see you like this, I wonder how you ever survived the wilderness alone for so long."

"I had no choice. It was survive or die."

"You speak of things so calmly. Was that how you kept your sanity?"

She shrugged. "Collapsing into a weeping heap would do me no good. I'd already been isolated by my clan for my wants and dreams. It wasn't too difficult a transition from being ignored to total isolation."

Orrick studied her delicate face, appreciating what had been revealed by a thorough cleansing. Her cheekbones seemed higher; her blue eyes appeared more warm than cool. But through it all, he saw strength and determination. "You would have been a magnificent warrior."

"I still am a warrior. Only in different clothing at present." She offered him a smile as she accepted his arm and allowed him to lead her into the great hall.

Orrick returned her smile. He liked seeing her like this— at ease and playful. His thoughts turned to tomorrow, wondering what she would be like as they trained to return her to full strength. As heat flooded his body once more, he forced his thoughts in a different direction. It would be best if he tucked his attraction to her away. Even if he might want it, nothing could come of an alliance between the two of them. Alastair would see to that.

ISOLDE STRAIGHTENED AND forced herself to remain calm as they approached the head table where the others were seated. Never in her life had she felt as elegant as she did in this moment. While at Scorrybreac, she'd never allowed her maid to do anything but plait her hair, and the clothes she'd chosen to wear had been more serviceable than stylish. As her full skirt swirled about her legs, Isolde imagined for just a moment that she was someone else—someone whose future could possibly contain wearing beautiful gowns, dining with beloved family members, and finding comfort in the arms of the well-bred man beside her, who was dark and handsome and fashionably attired in the MacLeod tartan. "What can I expect from tonight?"

"With my family, one never knows." He paused and turned to look at her. "You are safe with me."

At a nod from her, they entered the chamber. As the others turned towards them, at first there was shock on many of their faces as they appraised her from head to toe. Then they smiled. Gwendolyn and Fiona had transformed her into what others expected her to be. Their smiles, however, faded as she and Orrick drew nearer, and a heavy tension filled the air. Alastair's features darkened as Orrick held out the seat opposite Gwendolyn, before Orrick sat beside her.

As soon as they were seated, the cook and her staff began serving supper. There was little conversation directed at Isolde during the meal, for which she was thankful. Not being the focus of everyone's attention allowed her to eat in peace the best meal she'd had in a long while. The venison was marvellously flavourful and so tender, the slices of meat almost dissolved in her mouth. The meat was complemented with a celeriac, turnip, and beetroot gratin, a rosehip and crab-apple jelly, and claret. It was a simple meal, but sublime.

After everyone had finished eating, an apple tart was served and the wine glasses were topped off before the servers departed, leaving the family to talk amongst themselves. Relaxed and more sated than she'd been in a year, Isolde sat back and sipped her claret.

"How pleased we are that your fever is gone and that you could join us for supper," Gwendolyn said with a smile.

Isolde set her glass down, nervously studying the deep crimson of the wine as the light reflected through it. "Dinner was delicious. My compliments to Mrs Honey."

Gwendolyn smiled. "I will let her know that you liked the meal."

"Does your arm pain you much?" Alastair asked as he studied Isolde as though unable to reconcile the change in her appearance.

"I have no idea what is in the poultice Lottie puts on my wound every morning, but it leaves me with only minimal pain. I am looking forward to using my arm and my bow again tomorrow."

Farther down the table, Graeme set down his glass and frowned. "Are you ready for such activity yet? I advise the castle guards to wait at least a week after an injury before returning to practise."

"I do not have the luxury of time," Isolde replied, trying to keep her words light.

"Is there somewhere else you'd rather be?" Tormod asked with an arch of his brow.

A flicker of apprehension raced through Isolde. "It was never my intent to stay long."

"Where will you go?" Fiona asked with concern in her voice.

Isolde shrugged. "Perhaps I'll make my way to the mainland and head north. There are few English patrols the higher into the Highlands one gets, at least at present."

Alastair's gaze narrowed. "How would you know that?"

Isolde pressed her lips together as she looked about the table at all the curious gazes upon her. She should have guarded her thoughts and words more closely. Was it time to tell them the truth about herself? Lieutenant Collins had returned. If he stayed, then the MacLeods might very well need to know the intelligence she'd gathered in her two short months as a spy for the English crown.

She faced Orrick. It would be easier if she talked to him as she let the others in on her secret. "You asked about my life after leaving my brother's castle. I've lived a complicated life from that time until now."

She shuddered as she thought back to that day. "I left my home in a hurry, distraught and with so much emotion I didn't know that I'd wandered into a trap set by the English until it was too late. They captured me and held me prisoner. Lieutenant Collins—"

"Lieutenant Collins? The Englishman who was here earlier?" Alastair asked.

Isolde nodded. "He trained me to spy against my own

people by using my feminine wiles to get men to talk to me."

"He forced himself on you." Orrick swore under his breath.

Isolde shook her head. "He tried, but my *sgian-dubh* helped remind him to keep his distance."

Orrick's shoulders relaxed slightly as he waited expectantly for her to continue.

"For the first two weeks, during the day the English had me roaming the isle in an effort to obtain information on clan movements. They wanted to know of clan alliances and discord."

"Why did you tell them anything?" Alastair demanded.

She turned towards him and met his heated gaze. "Because they threatened the life of my brother, over and over. Not just to label him a Jacobite, but a traitor. John might have given up on me, but I would have done anything to protect him from those men. Since the reports I gave them contained little if any real information, I kept doing as they asked." Isolde swallowed roughly, returning her gaze to Orrick. "After they failed to gain any important information, they began to push me to betray my own people by reporting on activities and conversations within their households. As soon as my reports led to the imprisonment of the chief of Clan MacTavish, I fought for my escape."

"How did you manage that?" Orrick prompted.

"One night, a year or so ago, I turned my training on the Englishmen of the twenty-ninth regiment. Several of the men had gone to bed early that night, leaving only six of us in the dining tent. I encouraged the five men present to drink more than they should have. I flirted with them in the way they'd taught me, until I could get each of them away from the group. Once in their tents, I rendered them senseless, gagged them, then tied their wrists and ankles. One by one I picked them off until it was only me and Lieutenant Collins."

She swallowed roughly, but forced herself to continue. "Lieutenant Collins must have realised what I was doing because upon my return to the dining tent, he grabbed my arm and threw me to the ground. As he kicked me, accusing me of betrayal, I fell back on my warrior training and retaliated with a kick that slammed into his knee. When he regained his balance he attacked me again and again as I tried to defend myself. I was dizzy and bleeding when he came at me with both of his fists aimed at my head. That was when I reached for my *sgian-dubh* and stabbed him in the neck."

Isolde closed her eyes as she remembered the look of horror on the lieutenant's face as he reared back. Blood sprayed from his throat onto her dress before his eyes rolled back and he slumped forward onto her. She had been unable to hold back a scream as she'd struggled to free herself from his motionless body. "Until today, I thought he was dead. That I had killed him."

She opened her eyes and met Orrick's sympathetic gaze. "Lieutenant Collins is not a forgiving man. If he finds out you are sheltering me, he will attack with every resource available to him."

Orrick frowned. "You let my brothers and me worry about Lieutenant Collins and the English. Your goal right now is to regain your strength and the use of your bow arm."

Farther down the table, the youngest MacLeod brother, Callum, leaned forward with a grin. "Besides, we have the Fairy Flag on our side should things get out of hand with the English."

"We'll not be using the Fairy Flag to fight the English," Alastair countered, wiping the grin from his brother's youthful face.

"I'd like to help find a solution," Isolde said.

"My brothers and I can deal with this." Alastair crossed his arms over his chest.

Isolde straightened. "I've admitted to being a spy for the enemy. I left that behind."

Alastair's eyes narrowed. "How can we be certain of that?"

Orrick's frown deepened. "We all know what that is like. We've all left behind pieces of our past we did not like."

"I meant no offence," Alastair said, turning his heated gaze on Orrick. "But do we really know this woman? At least enough to let her help us?"

Isolde bristled. "Just because I am female doesn't mean I cannot help find a resolution to this problem."

Orrick's gaze shifted between Isolde and Alastair. "My

brother doesn't have a problem with strong females. Gwendolyn is proof of that. However, until Lieutenant Collins and his men are a problem we can no longer avoid, let us save our worrying for other things."

Isolde bit her lip, still concerned. "Do you think the lieutenant's return will be followed by more English troops? Will the isle clans object to that?"

"Once the news of the lieutenant's return makes its way through the clans, people will settle down and wait to see what happens next," Orrick said.

"That might be true," Rowena said as she stood up. "In the meanwhile, we have to protect ourselves from not only the English but also from Iso . . . Izzy."

Orrick's face clouded. "Sit down, Rowena, and rein in your sharp tongue. Our guest is not here to harm us. She needs our help."

"What utter nonsense," Rowena retorted. "Did you hit your head while you were out in the wilderness? We all know from experience that the men of our family become irrational when hit in the head." She narrowed her gaze on Isolde. "If you give that woman back her weapon on the morrow, you'll be sorry. Sarah Nicolson has always spoken of Izzy as temperamental, stubborn, hot-heated, and dangerous."

Orrick pushed his chair back roughly as he stood. "Watch your words, Rowena. Our father's past head injury is nothing to make light of. He became a tyrant after it happened. Besides, some could also say you are temperamental, stubborn, hot-heated, and dangerous." His gaze challenged his sister to dispute his claim.

Tormod scowled and stood. "Why are you so mad at Izzy, Rowena? Explain yourself so that we might all understand."

"I would love for her to explain why she left Scorrybreac Castle in the first place. All we've heard are stories she says were invented after she left." Rowena's eyes bored into Isolde's with a lethal mixture of fury and smugness.

The riveting stares from those around the table told Isolde she had no choice but to tell them that part of her tale.

Beside her, Orrick's jaw tightened. "You do not have to tell them anything you are not ready to reveal."

Isolde returned an appreciative smile that faded a moment later. "They have a right to know. My presence endangers the entire clan—not just from the English but from my brother as well." Isolde laced her fingers and studied them as she tried to decide where to start this part of her story. In the silence that descended over the chamber those who had stood took their seats once more, waiting.

"My father was a good man. When he realised he had a daughter who was more interested in swords than dolls, he encouraged me to follow my heart. He educated me alongside my brother during the afternoon. And every morning, he allowed me to spar with my brother and his friends at the castle."

Isolde paused as the memories crowded back. "I grew in

strength and spirit until I could not only match my brother's skill but exceeded it. When John switched his weapon of choice to the bow and arrow, then promptly discarded it, I picked up his bow and trained even harder. After years of training, my skill level was far superior to any other man in our clan, even John's."

Her heartbeat stumbled and again she paused, reining in her emotions. Retelling the story felt like she was reliving the events. "My father was about to approve my induction into the castle guard when he and my mother were called away on business. They sailed from Scotland to Flanders with a promise to return within the week, but their ship capsized during a storm, killing them both. John became the new laird, and refused to honour my father's wish that I be allowed to fight alongside the men. Instead he tried to marry me off.

"When it became clear to both John and Sarah that I wanted nothing to do with marriage, John came up with a plan. He invited the man he wanted me to marry to Scorrybreac and set up a challenge. If I could best Ewen MacPhee using my bow and arrows by hitting three targets he'd set up in the courtyard, I could join the guard. If I failed, then I would have no choice but to marry as my brother wished."

She shrugged and dropped her gaze to her hands. "I could have hit those targets with my eyes closed." She sighed. "To make an ugly story short, Ewen MacPhee cheated. He knocked into me and sent my rapidly fired arrows astray.

One arrow hit John and one hit my very pregnant sister-in-law in the belly, sending her into labour. I was forced out of the castle before I could learn whether or not Sarah or the child survived."

When she finished there was only silence. By some miracle, the twisting ache that had resided in her chest since she'd been cast out eased ever so slightly. Isolde looked up to see stunned expressions on the faces of those about the table.

Gwendolyn's hand drifted to her abdomen and rested there as though protecting the babe inside her. "Did no one at Scorrybreac take your side after witnessing these events?"

"Only my maid. I can only assume that everyone else was too afraid of what my brother would do to them if they stood against him. So I was cast as the villain and forced out of the castle."

Rowena's brows came together as though deep in thought. "Sarah never mentioned Ewen MacPhee, or targets. She told me you fired that arrow at her. That you shot directly at her."

"I would never harm an innocent or take the life of any child born or unborn." Isolde allowed herself a rueful smile. "I don't blame Sarah for any of her words against me. She was fighting for her life that day, and that of her child. She remembers the events of that day as they pertain to her survival."

Alastair studied her with a dark, probing gaze. "You are very forgiving considering what those events cost you."

Isolde regarded the laird suspiciously, not knowing if she had just been complimented or insulted.

"And despite my earlier reservations," he added with the hint of a smile, "I will allow you to train on the morrow, but only if you give your weapons back to Orrick when you are finished for the day."

"I can agree to that," Isolde replied, still wondering why he'd had a change of heart. Did he see the truth of her words? It mattered not. He had given her permission to train. For that she was more than grateful.

"Brea. The child's name is Brea." Rowena offered the words with a clearer brow.

Isolde held her breath. Was Rowena's sharing her niece's name with Isolde a peace offering? "Thank you, Rowena. Knowing her name means a lot to me."

"You're welcome. And thank you."

Isolde frowned. "For what?"

"For tonight. For telling all of us what must have been painful memories to dredge up."

To her horror, Isolde felt tears flood her eyes. Aye, the memories were hard to talk about, just as living on her own, with only herself and her bow for survival was difficult. Now being around people who seemed to not only understand but also accept her was difficult.

She looked about the table at the MacLeod clan. The laird and his brothers, their wives, brothers, sisters, and trusted guards. They now looked at her with some acceptance instead of complete defiance or suspicion. Perhaps they connected with her stories of betrayal, isolation, and resilience because they had suffered similar challenges in their lives as well. The thought brought a warmth to her chest that hadn't been there in a very long time.

This clan—the MacLeods—were survivors just like her.

CHAPTER NINE

I SOLDE ENTERED THE rear courtyard the next morning, dressed in another one of Rowena's gowns. This one was light and loose, allowing her to move her arms freely as she needed to when using her bow and arrow. The gown also did not cling to her legs, for which she was thankful. She'd broken her fast in her chamber with a Scotch egg and a brisk cup of tea. After revealing her darkest secrets last night, she wasn't certain she could face the rest of Orrick's family until she felt more like her old self: strong and in control.

Orrick entered the courtyard, carrying two swords. An eager smile crossed his handsome face. "Are you ready to begin?"

Disappointment curled Isolde's shoulders at the sight of the swords. "Where's my bow and quiver?"

He stopped before her and handed her a sheathed sword. "Your arm isn't ready for that weapon yet. Strength must come before you can fire one of your arrows correctly."

Was he being cautious because of the tale she'd told about hitting her brother and sister-in-law instead of a target? She supposed she couldn't blame him, but that didn't lessen the blow.

"First we must stretch." He held his own sheathed blade before him with one hand on the hilt and the other at the end of the protected blade. "Twist your arms to the left then the right as much as is possible before you feel a pull in the muscles of your left arm. We don't want to reopen your wound. And while you stretch, I want you to listen to the sounds around you as you become comfortable with your own body. Focus on the way it moves, the way your muscles glide, the way you connect with the ground below you."

Isolde scowled at him, wondering if he was serious. "How can such a thing help me prepare for battle?" Was he trying to make a fool of her as so many others had all her life?

There was no amusement in his expression. "We cannot fight for real or in a mock battle until we heal ourselves in both body and spirit."

She frowned. "You are training as well?"

He nodded as he stretched his arms back and forth. "I have every bit as much to gain from these lessons as you do if I ever intend to pick up a sword and battle again."

"Why would you have a hard time wielding a sword? Are you not a MacLeod? Your clan is known for their prowess in battle," she said while continuing to stretch, forcing her injured arm to move a little farther with each rotation.

Orrick straightened and his features pinched. "Not all MacLeods are warriors. And this one in particular has memories from battles in the West Indies that followed him home."

"Those memories must be very powerful to haunt you still." Isolde stopped stretching, wondering if she should reach out and comfort him. Something about the stiffness of his shoulders hinted at more than irritation. He was in pain from a source she could not see.

He closed his eyes briefly, heaving a deep sigh. "The memories haunt me both day and night." When he opened his eyes, they were filled with shadows. "I still see the faces of those whom I killed."

At his words, a strange ache came into her heart. "I'm sorry. That must be very hard." She brought her gaze to his.

He returned her gaze with an intense and knowing one. "No harder than having everyone in your life abandon you."

They were so alike, the two of them. Each carrying a burden that felt more like a snake in the back of their brains, waiting and watching. And when they least expected it, striking to remind them of the cruel trick life had played on them. "Will we ever break free from our pain?"

"Perhaps in time with new memories, happier memories, and much distance from the events in the past." Orrick offered her a sad smile. "For now, let us focus on the present and stretch in silence while keeping our memories at bay. Agreed?"

She returned his smile. "Agreed."

As the morning mist faded and the clouds overhead parted to reveal a glimmer of sunlight, silence surrounded the two of them. The only sounds Isolde could hear were the splash and retreat of the waves against the shore of Loch Dunvegan below the rear courtyard and the beat of her own heart. In the stillness something else came to her. The sensation yet again of someone watching her. Isolde studied her surroundings, but saw only Orrick. Should she mention something to him? Or was it only her imagination that had conjured such a feeling?

No sooner had that thought formed when a sudden chill came over her. A frothy grey mist swept across the courtyard then gathered into a more solid shape. The image of a woman appeared before Isolde. She unsheathed her weapon and held it before her. "What, by all that is holy, are you?"

Orrick didn't look frightened by the unusual event. In fact, he smiled at the apparition. "Mother. As usual, you come sliding in when we least expect you."

Isolde felt the blood drain from her face as she studied the swirling mist that had appeared from nowhere. "Your mother is a ghost?" Isolde couldn't keep the fear from her voice. Though the woman was nearly translucent, Isolde could make out her dark hair and soulful grey eyes. The apparition crept closer and a chill slithered across Isolde's skin.

"It's a long story, and one I will explain at another time. Right now, please allow me to introduce you. Isolde, this is my mother, Janet MacLeod. Mother, this is Izzy. She is staying with us for a few days until she regains her strength."

The girl is a danger.

The words resounded in Isolde's mind. Orrick seemed to hear them as well if his sudden frown were any indication.

"There is no need for concern, Mother. Izzy is a friend."

Isolde froze, her heart racing. She lowered her sword and studied the apparition. The woman's eyes had a familiarity about them. It was as if she were looking into Orrick's eyes. A multitude of questions filled her thoughts. How could his mother still be here if she had died? Did she die a violent death that somehow kept her suspended between this world and the next? Was this ghost the being she'd felt watching her over the past week?

As though sensing her thoughts, the ghost turned to Isolde. *I am only guilty of watching you with my son this morning. Anything else could not have been me, for I am tethered to the castle grounds. Even so, I can see much that others do not.*

Orrick moved to Isolde's side. His presence calmed her racing heart. "There is nothing to fear, Mother. We are all safe behind the thick walls of Dunvegan."

The apparition's brows knit. *I can sense danger, my son. It is closer than you think. Perhaps not from her, but because of her.*

"We know about the English troops' return to the isle. Alastair and Tormod are no doubt coming up with a plan for how to contain that threat."

Your brothers cannot fight this enemy alone. They will need your help.

Orrick made a soft sound of impatience. "I can no longer fight beside them, Mother. I lost that ability a few years ago. When I hold a sword in battle, I freeze. What happens if I go with them and cannot protect them as I should?"

You are resourceful, my son. You of all people know there are other ways to battle that do not include weapons. She looked down at the sword in his hands. *You seem able to hold a sword with no issue today.*

Orrick's lips thinned. "Only because I am training with Izzy."

Then train her more until you can fight with no fear. You'll need to do that again very soon, I sense.

With those words, the ghost disappeared, leaving an irritated Orrick behind. "My mother knows not of what she speaks."

"Has she come to you with such predictions before? You seemed very at ease in her presence, or at least more so than I was."

"She's predicted events that have happened in the past few months," he grumbled.

"And that makes you angry?"

"I don't know what it makes me." Orrick shoved his hand through his hair. "Though now I feel as though I need to run the length of the loch or ride hard and fast through the moors."

Isolde lifted her unsheathed sword in challenge. "A good sword fight always helps me to centre myself. Care to battle through your emotions with me?"

His gaze was uncertain. "Are you well enough to fight hard?"

She put her left arm behind her and her right foot forward. "I'm battling you with my uninjured arm. As long as you do not strike my left, then I'll be well." Isolde hid the pleasure she felt creeping up inside her. She'd longed to battle Orrick MacLeod again since she'd beaten him in armed combat six summers ago. "Do not go easy on me because I am a female. I can take anything you care to unleash upon me."

Challenge flashed in his eyes as he leapt forward, cutting and slashing as he advanced. He was angry. She could feel it with each blow she parried. She did not attack. Instead she allowed him to burn through his pent-up emotions. Only when his movements became more controlled did she press forward with a thrust and a twist of her arm. She caught his blade and sent it flying to the ground.

Orrick's eyes went wide. "I'd forgotten how good you were with a sword."

"Again?" she asked, handing him back his fallen sword.

He accepted it, and with a salute came at her once more. Their blades clashed again and again, the clink of steel creating a rhythmic sound that reverberated through the morning air. As Isolde fought, a renewed sense of purpose flowed through her. For the past year she had only been a hunter. Today, she proved she was a warrior once more.

Orrick was strong. His strikes might have taken her down had she not been light on her feet. That was an asset some men never seemed to understand. They had the advantage physically, but she could move in ways they could not. She tossed her plaited hair over her shoulder, allowing Orrick one last pass before she pressed her attack with renewed vigour. She swiped her sword. He countered. She stepped closer and, with a twist of her arm and a nudge from her knee, she brought him to the ground at her feet.

He lay against the grass looking up at her with no anger, only a smile. "I would say your right arm is as steady as it ever was."

She offered him her hand. He grasped it and allowed her to haul him to his feet. "Next time," she said, "try balancing more on the balls of your feet and keep your shoulders centred over your hips. That will help you use your strength against me."

"Giving me tips on how to defeat you?" He laughed. "I've never met a woman like you."

She recoiled as if he had slapped her as his words echoed those she'd heard all her life from some men. *You're an abomination. Why can't you be a normal female? You should learn your true place in this world.* Isolde stepped back, putting some much-needed distance between them.

Orrick was just like everyone else. She had hoped that

perhaps something else would develop between them—a camaraderie, a friendship. They were two injured warriors who needed to be whole once more. His words proved he was just like the other men in her life. He was not her friend and he never would be.

ORRICK WATCHED THE pleasure drain from Isolde's face at his words. Pain crept into her wide blue eyes and a shell of aloofness came about her once more. "I did not mean my words as an insult. Nay. You are a skilled warrior. Any army would be lucky to have you amongst their ranks."

The woman was tough and very good with a sword. Much better than he could ever hope to be, even with her helpful suggestions. So why was it her brother had cast such a talented warrior aside? Was it his own pride that caused the rift between them even before the accident? He'd seen enough of battle to know that a man's self-regard was often the difference between life and death.

But Orrick was not like most men. He'd grown up in the shadows of Alastair and Tormod. He had always been the third-best child, brother, and eventually warrior as the castle residents were only too willing to inform him. Unwittingly, he'd done the same thing to Isolde. He'd hurt her. He found no pleasure in the thought. And he refused to allow the new rift between them to continue. "I apologise if my words upset you. I should have realised you had to fight harder than anyone else to prove you are worthy. If you are willing, I would like to continue to train with you."

"With me? A female?" A dark expression crossed her face, then vanished.

"Aye. I had thought I would be training you, but in that I was wrong. It is your skill and prowess that just might help me regain my will to fight once more."

Her features lightened with a hint of pleasure. "Sometimes it is not skill that will see you through. It is the reason for which you are fighting. If the cause is just, then it is easy to pick up a sword. If not, then the task is that much harder."

He stepped closer and his heart beat a little faster. Despite their workout, she smelled like the morning mist mixed with the scent of the sea and a hint of Scottish rose, the combination fresh and intoxicating. "Shall we train some more?"

"Have you not had enough battles for one day?"

He shook his head and smiled. "We'll switch to shooting arrows at targets, instead of you forever landing me on my backside."

A hint of a smile returned to her lips. At the sight, warmth flared inside him. "When well, I can always best you with my arrows," she said with a challenge in her voice.

"Come, you've proven to me that your arm is ready for more physical exertion. I set up targets in the gardens outside the gates. There's plenty of space to move the targets as far away as we'd like."

Her smile slipped. "I doubt moving the targets will be necessary. Simply supporting the bow as I draw the bowstring will be enough of a challenge at first."

They walked into the castle and headed to the armoury. The room on the ground floor near the barracks was filled with swords, targes, lances, pikes, bows, crossbows, long bows, pole and battle axes, daggers of all sizes, and pistols. If war ever came to Dunvegan, the MacLeods would be well armed.

"Where is my bow and quiver?" Isolde asked as she looked about the chamber.

Even he would have been hard-pressed to pick the single wooden weapon out of the collection if he hadn't been the one to hang it on the stone wall. Orrick stepped up to the hook near the middle of the chamber and took her bow down, handing the weapon to Isolde. "Your bow is well made and nicely waxed. How did you manage to maintain it while you were in the wilderness?"

"'Tis not wax but tree sap that I used to keep it supple. I gathered what I could to maintain both the bow and the string," she said, hitching her quiver over her shoulder.

Orrick armed himself with a bow and a quiver, and led the way outside, then over the drawbridge towards the garden. The morning mist had faded and overhead the sun fought to break through the clouds, leaving splashes of dappled light on the long stretch of grass on the southern side of the creek that fed Loch Dunvegan.

"I set out two targets." He pointed at two piles of hay more than fifty feet away. "It should help us to have something to aim at."

"First I must see if I can string my bow." She set her quiver on the ground. It took three tries before she could finally bend the bow and slip the loop at the string's end into the notch at the top.

"How is your arm?" Orrick asked, feeling compassion rise within him at the effort it had taken her to string her bow.

"There is only minimal pain." Next she held the bow in her left hand, relaxing and extending her arm as though trying to reacquaint herself with the bow's weight.

"You are doing well," Orrick said.

"The hard part hasn't even begun yet." Her eyes were overbright as she drew one of her arrows. She carefully set the string onto the nock slit. Supporting the arrow with one finger on the string above it, two below, she pulled the string to touch her lips and chin. She had to shift her grip several times to balance the arrow correctly. And even so, Orrick could visibly see her arm trembling at the strain. Any movement whatsoever could affect the aim of an arrow.

When she released the arrow, Orrick could not hold back a sharp intake of breath as the arrow wobbled and careened several feet to the right. She let her bow arm fall to her side as her composure faltered.

"Let's go again." He tried to keep his voice light.

"To what purpose?" Beside him, she took a deep, shaking breath.

He stepped closer. "Were you able to fire an arrow accurately the first time you ever tried?"

"Nay."

He saw uncertainty in her eyes, but he ignored it as he drew an arrow from her quiver. "Then why do you expect perfection now? Come. Let's try again. This time, I'll help you hold your arm steady." He came around behind her and placed his hand on the bow below hers, lifting it towards the hay. He handed her the arrow.

She nocked it and worked to balance the weight as he felt the warmth of her body merge with his, and with it a thrill of anticipation. "Does that feel more stable?"

"Aye." Her breath caught as she touched the string to her lips.

His heart raced as he watched the bowstring caress the softness of her full, pink lips. Orrick shook his head and tried without success to pull his gaze away from her mouth. He was here to help her regain her strength, not find pleasure. And yet, he couldn't help but wonder if the woman's intensity for battle would spill over into other areas of her life.

At the thought, arousal roared through him. He gave up trying to look away and continued his exploration. Her simple golden-brown dress accentuated her breasts and hips as the fabric skimmed across her shapely form. To some she might appear soft and feminine, but Orrick knew the strength and determination that her flowing gown concealed. She was a dangerous warrior whether dressed in fine lace or a cloak of pelts.

A quick intake of her breath brought him back to the moment as her fingers opened and the arrow flew straight into the hay. The sound of the impact told him the strike had been both true and strong. "Success," he said, lifting his hand to capture one of the tendrils of her golden hair that had escaped her plait during their earlier battle. He twined it about his finger.

She half-turned, glancing back at him. It was all the invitation he needed. He leaned forward and placed his lips against hers. His breath quickened as he deepened the kiss. Her right hand edged around his nape, and her fingers sifted through his hair. When her tongue caressed his, he moaned with a longing he could not name, a longing that urged him to capitulate. He would surrender to her every day if these reckless sensations were a part of their battles.

"Nay," she gasped, drawing back.

Orrick shifted her head down against the frantic hammering of his heart. "I did not mean to do that," he breathed against the softness of her hair.

She stepped back out of his embrace. "That is probably enough practise for today." She touched her lips with the back of her hand.

"How is your arm?"

She dropped her arm to her side. "I think it's improving. A few more strengthening sessions and I should be able to hit a target without your assistance." Confusion clouded her gaze. "Then again, perhaps I should train alone and then leave this place."

"Why is it you want to leave so badly? What awaits you out there besides danger and pain?" He saw fear flit through her eyes.

"It's what I must do," she said before she turned and fled.

If she left, then he would return to the man he'd become over the last few years even though he longed to be something more. His memories of the West Indies kept holding him back. He'd at one time been the third-best warrior at Dunvegan when it came to swordsmanship, though he excelled above them both with a bow. Or did that even matter now that he couldn't use either?

Alastair and Tormod had moved on with their lives since returning to Dunvegan. They'd fallen in love and had married women who were their equals. Yet Orrick was trapped by his memories.

Isolde might think she needed to leave, but Orrick desperately wanted her to stay. For she was the only one who made him feel hope for a different future.

CHAPTER TEN

I SOLDE RACED TOWARDS the castle with her bow in hand. She didn't really want to go back inside just yet. She needed time to herself to figure out what had happened. Orrick had kissed her. Yet it was her own response that left her unsettled.

Instead of heading to the gates, she followed the creek down to the shore until she stood before Loch Dunvegan. She drew in a breath of the cool winter air, then closed her eyes and pressed her lips together, trying to block out the memory of Orrick's kiss.

When the action failed to bring calm to her heavy and confused soul, she opened her eyes and looked out at the peaceful waters that rippled at her feet. She drew another deep breath and studied the life that teemed on the salt loch. Seals poked their heads above the water, staring at her while seabirds chattered amongst themselves as they floated on the wind. She rolled her left shoulder back and forth. If only the burning ache would ease, she would leave this place and never look back.

Weariness invaded her limbs. Who was she kidding?

Now that she had retasted all the luxuries of life she'd given up, it would be hard to go back to her cave. Here at Dunvegan she had warmth, food in greater variety, shelter, and clothing she didn't have to make herself. She reached up and ran a hand through the loose tendrils of her hair as Orrick had done only moments ago. She knew she should not want or even allow herself to feel the desire that had consumed her as his lips met hers.

In that moment she'd felt the power of his desire and a startling stab of her own. She knew the best thing to do would be to stay away from him. She'd seen that kind of desire before in others and knew where it led. Such feelings would be harder to leave behind than anything else. But there was no other choice.

Or, was there? Perhaps she could stay at Dunvegan. Live her life behind its solid walls, safe from the English by never leaving again. A heartbeat later, the usual heaviness on her shoulders returned. Her presence at Dunvegan would cost the MacLeods an alliance with her brother's clan. Isolde clenched her right hand in her skirt, feeling absurdly lost. She sighed, the sound as torn as it felt. In another time and another place perhaps there could have been something between them, but not now. Not ever. And even as she told herself she was doing the right thing, all she could think about was how much she wanted to kiss Orrick again.

ARIA SLIPPED PAST the guards as she followed Isolde inside the gates of Dunvegan. The guards were too busy watching a distressed Isolde run through the gates and into the castle to pay much notice to a dark shape that appeared more like a shadow than anything else. It wasn't long before Aria found her way inside the mighty fortress. She was weary of observing from a distance. What better way to truly know when she should reveal herself to them and make her offer to return the lost child to the MacLeods.

Now that she was inside, she would need to find a place to hide and watch the MacLeods as they went about their daily lives. Once again, patience would be her friend. It might take a few days to determine how best to approach them. But what were a few more days when compared to the lifetime she'd already waited?

FOR THE NEXT three days Isolde managed to keep her distance. She stayed in her chamber, mostly. She took her meals there by herself because while the others' attitudes had thawed towards her somewhat, there was still much tension in the castle that she no doubt had caused.

Lottie was the only person she allowed to enter her chamber. The healer came every day to clean and redress Isolde's wound. Yesterday Lottie stopped applying the poultice since Isolde's skin was no longer singed. Two dark pink scars stood out against her pale flesh, ribbons of colour that would forever remind her of the man she'd encountered in the wilderness. Despite the scars, her wounds were healing and she was healthy. It wouldn't be long now before she was fully healed.

To make certain she was ready for that day, Isolde practised holding her bow and drawing the string back for hours in her chamber. She did not need to shoot an arrow to regain her strength. Once the bow felt less cumbersome in her hands, then she would add an arrow to make certain she had not lost her accuracy.

On the fourth day after she and Orrick had shared a passionate kiss, she ventured out of her chamber after breaking her fast. Lottie had assured her it was a time when Orrick was usually in the library reading. The healer also divulged that Orrick was a scholar, having brought back many books from his time away in Spain and the West Indies. He spent hours reading in the library every day, which meant it was safe for Isolde to venture into the armoury again to retrieve more arrows.

Carefully dressed in the golden-brown dress Rowena had let her borrow, with her hair neatly plaited and hanging down her back, Isolde crept down the staircase, careful to keep her steps light.

"Good morning."

The quietly spoken salutation was so unexpected, Isolde gasped and nearly tripped on the stair. In a heartbeat, Orrick was beside her. His hand wrapped around her good arm until he was certain she'd regained her footing, and even when she had, he left it there. Warmth curled in her stomach at the sight of him. They had only been apart a few days, but she'd forgotten the way his linen shirt clung to his wide shoulders and the muscles that lay sculpted beneath. The features of his face brightened and a light came to his eyes when he smiled down at her.

Her breath caught as she stared at him in mute fascination. The muscles of her mouth and throat struggled to form words, to say something intelligible. When she could not, she gave up and greeted him with a simple: "Good day."

"Are you feeling better? You must be if you are venturing out of your chamber. We've missed you the last four days."

Isolde swallowed roughly at his nearness. "I apologise. I needed time—"

"There is no need for apology. You've been through an ordeal. No one would raise an eyebrow if you did not appear for another two weeks."

Isolde laced her fingers together. "I am not so weak as that."

"Good. Then prove it to me by sparring with me."

She drew herself up. "Right now?"

Orrick responded with a smile. Not just any smile. A disarming smile. One that made her legs feel weak. No one had ever smiled at her like that before. "Seems like as good a time as any, wouldn't you agree? Besides, I'll not give you a chance to retreat to your chamber again."

She wanted to object, but he was right. She had not only retreated. She was hiding as much from him as she was from herself. "Swords or bows? If bows, I do not have that weapon with me."

"We already know your skill far outweighs my own with a sword. Let us stick to the bow. Perhaps I will have a chance to best you at that." He tucked her arm through his and escorted her back upstairs to her chamber, where she collected her bow and quiver.

"I was on my way to the armoury to get more arrows when you came upon me. Should we gather more before we go outside?"

"Everything we need is outside waiting for us. I made certain of that earlier."

"You knew I would leave my chamber today?"

He smiled at her again and her pulse quickened. "You had to leave sometime. I've been waiting for you for the past four days." The husky baritone of his voice warmed her more than the cloak he settled about her shoulders before they stepped outside and made their way to the rear courtyard. He'd moved the hay piles inside the keep and had hung targets made from coiled straw in the middle of them. "Do you like this? I measured and the distance is fifty feet away if we stand here." He stopped behind a row of shells he'd set on the grass.

He'd gone to a lot of trouble on her behalf. "It's perfect," she said, drawing a shaky breath, trying to still the rapid beat of her heart. No one had ever done anything to try to please her before. The knowledge that he had did strange things to her insides. She quickly attached her string to her bow and drew an arrow from her quiver. The familiar activity helped take her mind off the man beside her for a moment at least. "Ready?" She was suddenly eager to see if her strengthening exercises had been enough to help her shoot with more accuracy than she had before.

"Care to make this interesting?" He stepped closer and she could feel the intensity of his gaze upon her.

Isolde frowned. "What did you have in mind?"

He brought a finger to her mouth, tracing the sensitive outline of her lips, moving slowly across the top, then the bottom. "If I best you, I get to choose a reward. If you win, you get to do the same."

No man had ever touched her in such a way before. Her mouth tingled as she fought the urge to lean into his pleasurable touch. "It is highly unlikely that you could win this challenge."

"Shall we begin?"

"Aye." She stepped back, forcing him to drop his hand. "Let the challenge begin," she said, suddenly determined to win. What boon would she ask for? Or what favour would she be forced to give? Her heart raced in her chest as she nocked her arrow and sighted the target in the distance.

Or would she win either way? Because suddenly all her

thoughts centred not on the red bullseye of the target but on Orrick's smiling lips.

***

ISOLDE'S FIRST ARROW went wide, not hitting the target or the hay. Her features steeled as she sent a second arrow towards the target. This one hit the edge of the target, but her quick release of breath told him she was disappointed. "That's not bad," he said, trying to cheer her up. "That's why we are practising. It will take time to get back to the markswoman you were before."

He fired two arrows at the target, intentionally aiming for the outer rings. When it was her turn to shoot again, he watched her raise her bow and nock her next arrow. He had spent the last four days waiting for her to emerge from her chamber, and the last four nights contemplating the ceiling of his own. He was seized by madness. What else could explain the longing that had taken hold of him? The moment his lips had touched hers, some of the doubts that had assailed him since his return to Dunvegan had fled. He'd felt a sense of belonging, with a renewed vigour for life.

The words she'd said before running to her chamber came back to him. 'Sometimes it is not skill that will see you through. It is the reason for which you are fighting. If the cause is just, then it is easy to pick up a sword.' If he had to protect Isolde from harm, he might once again become the warrior he had been before the West Indies.

"It is your turn," Isolde's voice interrupted his thoughts. She scowled at him. "You seem far away in thought. Are you certain you wish to continue with our challenge?"

"Absolutely." Orrick was caught and held by the brightness of her blue eyes. Those eyes showed no fear, betrayed no vulnerability, though he knew she must be terrified of not regaining her prior skill. A quick glance at the target revealed she had yet to hit the centre.

He fired two arrows, hitting the inner rings of the target before stepping back to observe her again.

She captivated him in a way no other woman ever had. While brandishing a sword, her movements had been tightly controlled, graceful, and yet elegant. She proved she had power and strength, but not at the cost of her femininity. While holding a bow, he could see the outline of the well-honed muscles in her arms, shoulders, and back. And while she appeared stronger than any woman he'd ever met, a softness, a suppleness existed also. He'd had proof of that when he'd pulled her body close to his while trying to stave off her chills.

She was feminine strength. An odd yet alluring combination. "You said your father allowed you to train with his other guards. How old were you when you started?"

She raised her bow, and with only a slight hesitation replied, "Six."

"You were challenging adult males at six years of age?"

He couldn't keep the incredulousness from his voice.

She paused and turned to face him. "I sparred with my brother, John, and his friends until I was eight, then I started battling the younger warriors before moving on to the older ones."

"You've been a warrior your whole life."

She tipped her head, and the loose tendrils that had worked free of her plait touched her cheek. In the morning light, her hair shone like spun silk.

"When did you and your brothers start to train?" Isolde asked.

Orrick focused on the curve of her red lips as she took her next shot. "Not until we were twelve. My mother was determined that we focus on our lessons before we distracted ourselves with battles."

Isolde nodded. "That was wise of her. Once you start battling, it seems to never stop." She lowered her bow. "May I ask you a question about your mother?" At his nod, she asked, "How is it she became a ghost?"

Orrick looked away from her, inhaling to try to regain his focus. "Who really knows? She died a horrible death at my father's hands. Most of her children suspect it's because she's protecting us from something."

"Can she do anything physical to help protect you?"

Orrick nodded, looking at her once more. "She can move objects with her mind, but that is it. Mostly, she feels when someone in the castle is in danger and can give us advance warning."

Isolde's mouth slightly opened as amazement filled her eyes. "That can be helpful, at least. Even a moment of advance warning can make the difference between life and death sometimes."

He didn't want to talk about his mother or why she was here. With a sudden urgency, he wanted to win this competition. "Enough delaying. We'd best get back to our match. I believe it is still your turn to shoot."

Isolde shook her head in mock exasperation before she smiled. "You were the one distracting me." Her gaze moved to meet his and she motioned her hand for him to step back. "If you will kindly stand over there, I might actually hit the target."

She had admitted that his presence distracted her. The thought made him smile in return. This time when she shot her arrow, it hit the inner ring, moving ever closer to the bullseye. She groaned. "What is wrong with me? I used to be able to hit dead on whatever target I wanted."

"You'll get back there with practise," he said, trying to sound encouraging. "You are holding your own against me."

She drew her brows together and regarded him with a serious expression. "You are not shooting your best to try and spare my feelings. I wish you would be honest and put all your skill into this contest."

"You want me to win?"

She narrowed her gaze. "I want you to treat me like a

true competitor."

He released a breath as he drew an arrow from his quiver and prepared to shoot. This time, he perfected his aim and sent the arrow flying towards the target. The arrow hit the centre just as he nocked a second arrow that soon joined the first. He had won whatever game he and Isolde were playing.

When he turned to Isolde, she tried to hide any emotion, but he saw much in the lines of her face. "You won. What boon do you ask?"

He set his bow on the ground then moved to stand before her. "I would have a kiss. A real kiss. Not a peck on the lips."

A look of resolve settled on her face as she brought her right hand to his chest. In her left hand she clutched her bow. "I made a promise and I never go back on my word."

At her touch, warmth flared through his chest and his gaze fell to her lips. She looked up into his eyes and rose up on her toes. His heart pounded. He could feel the whisper of her breath against his mouth. The kiss hung motionless in the air between then, waiting for him to either bend down or her to press forward. That was all it would take to bring their lips together. When he could wait no longer, he closed his eyes and leaned down.

Her lips were soft and tasted sweet, like honeyed wine. The shape of her mouth fit perfectly against his. As she returned his kiss, his world began to tilt. A powerful onslaught of sensation flooded him, and he pulled her closer until he could feel the rapid flutter of her heart against his own. He slid his hands up to cup her face and deepened the kiss.

Her bow thumped to the ground. Her left hand crept up to his shoulder. The fingers of her right hand curled around his shoulder. Lost to his desire for her, he swept inside her mouth, aching for her to do the same. When she did, heat roared through him to centre in his loins. He pressed against her, needing to feel her against the most male part of himself.

She answered his need by moulding her body to his, and moaned. The fire between them swelled, pulling them into a dark, whirling storm of yearning and need. Their shared passion was carnal and fierce, blinding them to everything around them except each other.

He should have thought to ask for her kiss abovestairs, where they would have as much privacy as they desired, where they could allow instinct to take them where it would.

The sound of a throat clearing nearby cut through Orrick's raging desire. He ended the kiss abruptly at the sound.

Isolde stiffened against him. She pressed a hand to his chest as hot colour rose to her cheeks.

Instead of releasing her and letting her fall to the ground on legs that were most likely as unsteady as his own, Orrick held firm, trying to be an anchor in the storm that was slowly releasing its grip.

Alastair studied the two of them with a raised brow and a sly grin. "Am I interrupting? Clearly I am, so don't bother with an answer."

"What do you want?" Orrick asked, grateful that his voice sounded steadier than he felt.

"Our scouts have returned and report that the village of Roag is being attacked."

"By the MacQueens? The MacDonalds?"

"We don't know anything more than that the raid has begun and that the villagers need our help," Alastair explained.

Orrick's stomach hardened to a knot. "What is your plan?" He relaxed his grip on Isolde so that she could ease away from him when she was able. A heartbeat later, she shifted away, then bent to retrieve her bow before stepping several feet away. She tugged at her skirt to straighten it about her hips.

"The men are assembling in the front courtyard. I want you to join us." Alastair's features pinched.

Only moments ago, Orrick's blood had flowed with molten heat. Now it turned ice cold. "I cannot. I'll be no help in battle, Alastair. Besides, do you truly need me when you have two hundred well-trained guards to attend you, and many more in training?"

"Aye. We need you. The three of us always ride into battle together. Our connection as triplets helps us to anticipate each other's moves."

"Who will lead the clan if we are all slaughtered?" Orrick asked.

"Callum will remain here. His skill as a warrior is growing daily, and he kept the castle and the men in order after Father's death. I daresay he could do so again."

"I'm not ready," Orrick objected.

Alastair's hands went to his hips. "I saw you strike that target with your last two arrows. If you cannot use a sword, then bring your bow or take a pistol, or both. I need you beside me along with Tormod. Together the three of us are stronger than we are apart."

Orrick shut his eyes, then realised his mistake as the faces of those he'd killed came back to him in vivid detail. He flinched and opened his eyes. "I don't know if I can, Brother. I cannot seem to escape my memories."

"'Tis all right, Orrick." A feminine voice cut through the tension. "When the cause is just . . ."

His gaze lit on Isolde.

Her cheeks pale now, she straightened. "I will go and fight for the MacLeods."

She wasn't ready for battle. Granted, she'd bested him time and again with her sword, but that was while they were sparring. Every battle he'd ever been in held many elements of surprise and was no place for someone who was not fully healed. He was about to object, when Alastair stepped forward.

"Nay. I'll not take someone who puts my own men in danger because she is not at her physical peak."

"It's because I am female?"

"It's because you are injured." He pointed at the target in the distance—at the irrefutable evidence that lay before her. "Would you take a warrior with you into battle who could not defend herself or any of those around her?"

She swallowed roughly. "Nay. I would not."

"Then stay here with my pregnant wife and all the others who may have need of your comfort while I am gone with my brothers."

After a slight hesitation, she nodded. "I can do that."

Satisfied with Isolde's answer, Alastair turned to face Orrick. "Will you step into the role the three of us are destined to play as Guardians of the Isles? Our people need us."

What could he say that wouldn't make him look or feel like a coward? He gave Alastair a tight nod. God help him, against his better judgement, he was headed into battle once more.

CHAPTER ELEVEN

T HE LATE-MORNING SUN washed the front courtyard in hues of gold and grey. Isolde watched as the men departed. The thunder of hoofbeats echoed in the emptiness of her heart as the castle's men hurried to engage the enemy. Alastair had taken a hundred and sixty warriors with him to fight two potential clans but also perhaps the English. Now that the English were back, they could not be discounted as a potential threat. This was what she'd trained for her whole life—helping to protect the people of Scotland—but she would be denied that honour because of her inability to shoot her arrows as she had before.

Isolde stood with her back straight, not moving until the gates were closed and the drawbridge closed. The joy she had experienced over the last several days ebbed from her as she curled her empty left hand at her side. Her quiver and bow were safely tucked upstairs in her bedchamber. She'd have no need of the weapon here, inside the mighty walls of Dunvegan. Or perhaps ever again if her arm did not heal well. She could feel the cool aloofness she'd been forced to wear as a cloak in the wilderness come over her once more. An outcast was what she was, and it was time for her to own up to that fact. Whether she was ready or not, it was time to leave and resume her shadowed life.

She could be gone before Orrick and his brothers returned. And this time, no one would ever find her again—not animal, man, or the English. Her experiences over the last year had taught her many things about being invisible. It was time to put those skills to use.

As she headed inside the castle, her heart would have been heavy had she allowed emotion to slip through her newly erected barrier. It would be best if she left a note for Gwendolyn and Alastair, thanking them for her care. And a separate note for Orrick, explaining her decision. Then she wouldn't have to say goodbye. Isolde could leave, and eventually they would forget all about her.

She, however, would remember Orrick for the rest of her life, and especially the kiss they'd shared earlier. Just the thought of him brought a curl of heat to her core. The feel of his hands in her hair and tracing the curves of her back, his lips sliding against her own, the taste of him on her tongue, were all branded into her memory.

After gathering paper, ink, and a quill, Isolde hurried up the stairs to her bedchamber. The sooner she left, the better it would be for them all.

Isolde had just finished with her letters when a frothy grey mist slithered beneath the doorway. The mist gathered, then coalesced into the shape of a woman, her image growing more solid with each passing moment.

The castle is in danger.

The words resounded in Isolde's head as she stared at the woman before her. Even in her ghostly form, Isolde could see fear in Orrick's mother's eyes. "What do you mean, in danger?"

Someone comes. There is anger in his heart. And someone inside these walls will unknowingly betray the clan.

Isolde tensed, wondering how the woman could know such things. But who was she to argue with someone from the spirit realm? "Why come to me? Alastair left guards behind."

You pretend you do not, but you care about this castle and her people. You might make the difference in the heat of the moment.

Frustration swelled. "Your son has deemed I am not healed and am unsafe to battle around his people."

What were you just telling my son, Orrick? 'If the cause is just . . .'

A commotion sounded from outside in the courtyard below. Isolde hurried past the apparition to the window. She threw back the shutters to see Lieutenant Collins and his men advancing over the drawbridge. Her heart sank. Who had allowed them to enter while the laird and his men were away?

Isolde closed the shutters and turned to stare at the Grey Lady, trying to decide what to do. Should she sound the alarm and gather the remaining soldiers? Or was Lieutenant

Collins here for peaceful reasons? She discarded the thought immediately. From her experiences, she knew the man did not have a peaceful bone in his body. He was up to something—and that something had been perfectly timed so that Alastair and his brothers would be away from Dunvegan.

Isolde returned her gaze to the ghost. "You are right to come to me. I must stop the lieutenant, even if it means exposing my presence here."

A loud bang sounded belowstairs, a sound that was much closer than it should have been. Swallowing the tightness constricting her throat, Isolde grabbed her bow and strung it, then threw her quiver over her shoulder and headed for the door.

She made it to the landing of the stairs and was surprised to see four English soldiers halfway up the steps with their swords at the ready.

"Where is the laird's wife?" yelled the man in the front.

Isolde didn't think. She let instinct take over. She had arrow to string and flying before the men took another step. The arrow hit the first Englishman in the chest. He reared back then tumbled down the stairs. A second, third, and fourth arrow followed, all hitting their targets with a precision she had not been able to find earlier that day, despite the trembling in her bow hand. Four more men came up behind those who had fallen. With a roar of outrage, they charged.

Isolde drew her arrows and sent them flying, eliminating

three of the newest targets as they advanced. But one man surged closer while she'd been firing at the others. He was too close to strike with an arrow, so instead, she gripped her bow and struck him in the head with the upper limb. When he clutched his head, bellowing in pain, she kicked him in the gut as hard as she could, sending him tumbling down the stairs. He landed at the bottom of the staircase and lay motionless.

Behind her, Rowena and Gwendolyn burst from their chambers. "What is going—" Rowena's words died on her tongue as four more Englishmen charged up the stairs. She grabbed Gwendolyn by the arm and thrust her pregnant sister-in-law behind her back. "Merciful heavens!"

Staying focused on the attackers, Isolde drew an arrow and fired, then another. She would soon be out of arrows. What then? No sooner had the thought occurred to her, when a chill slithered across Isolde's flesh and a scraping sound came to her ears. Out of the corner of her eye, she saw the Grey Lady advancing, moving a broadsword across the floor with her mind. In that moment, Isolde was extremely grateful that the ghost was on her side.

Isolde fired off her last two arrows, then bent to retrieve the sword. To Rowena and Gwendolyn she said, "Go back in your chamber and bolt the door. Lady Janet, keep them safe," she said to the ghost as she picked her way down the stairs over the fallen men.

Three more men entered the open doorway and charged

up the stairs. One man was faster than the others. She recognised him as Silas from her time amongst them. He paused for a moment when he saw her. "You're alive?" A heartbeat later his features hardened. "Where is the laird's wife?"

"I'll never tell."

Silas gave a fierce growl as he came at her, slashing in an arc towards her head. Isolde easily blocked the blow. When Silas came at her again, their swords crashed, the sensation reverberating through her body. She ignored the pain in her left arm and pressed her attack.

"It seems fitting that I should finish you off after you tied me up and left me humiliated in my tent. Your new friends cannot help you now."

Isolde stared at the man, torn between anger and mirth and fear. They'd left her no choice but to tie them up so that she could escape. Just as she had no choice now about sending these men to their maker. Silas lunged, and she spun to the left before coming back around with an undercut that caught him off guard. He screamed as her sword swept along his abdomen. He dropped his weapon and clutched his injured midriff, then fell back, allowing the other two men to advance.

She assumed her fighting stance as the two men came closer. She focused on the enemy, determined not to let these men past her so they could get to Gwendolyn. No doubt they intended to kidnap the laird's wife and hold her hostage until Alastair declared his fealty to the English king. Only Isolde stood in the way of letting that happen.

The two men she recognised as Jasper and Henry. Their gazes locked with hers as they slashed violently at her. She stumbled back, catching herself before she fell. She twisted right, evading a blow that could have easily taken her leg. Even so, the two men fighting together forced her backwards. They bared their teeth, showing their delight.

In the next moment, Rowena was beside her, wielding her own weapon and dressed in a leather garment that fitted her body like a glove. No longer did she wear a skirt, but breeches. Her sword struck out, deflecting Henry's blow while Isolde turned to confront Jasper. Metal to metal, their swords rang a peal of power and violence until the two men lay defeated.

In the momentary silence, Isolde heard the familiar sounds of battle coming from the courtyard where the castle's men had engaged the English who had not made it through the castle doorway. Isolde turned to Rowena. "Return abovestairs and protect Gwendolyn at all costs."

"What about you?" Rowena asked breathlessly.

"I must help the guards." She took a step towards the door before Rowena caught her arm, forcing her to turn back towards the young woman.

"Before you go . . ." Rowena's features filled with remorse. "I was so wrong about you. Please, forgive me."

"There is nothing to forgive," Isolde said, stepping away.

Protecting those she cared for was what she'd been trained to do. She clutched her sword and emerged into the courtyard as the sound of battle filled the air. "It is time to show these Englishmen what a Scottish lass is made of." Isolde shifted her weight onto the balls of her feet and prepared as two men rushed towards her.

For a moment, her gaze shifted to something moving along the tower on her left. A woman dressed in a white, flowing gown, with a gold band at her hips, stood between one of the crenellations and aimed a bow at the warriors below. Who was this woman? Was she friend or foe?

In the next moment, an arrow struck the chest of the man before her. Then another arrow followed, hitting another Englishman. Who she was didn't matter as much as the fact she appeared to be on the MacLeod side. With a quick nod of approval, Isolde turned back to the battle before her just as two men charged.

Isolde dispatched first one then the other, but two more replaced the fallen Englishmen. Lieutenant Collins must have brought the entire company with him this time. As if her thoughts had conjured him up, he appeared out of the corner of her eye, fighting the castle guards. Isolde attacked the two men before her, until they lay at her feet. She drew a tight breath, trying to determine where her help was needed most amongst those who still fought, when Lieutenant Collins saw her. His eyes flared in surprise that quickly slid to anger, even hatred.

"I thought I saw you at the window the other day, but I dismissed what I saw as an illusion created by the snow and the chilling cold." The lieutenant's mouth curved into a lethal smile. "It will be an added bonus to kill you this day while also taking the laird's wife hostage."

A cold sickness settled in the pit of Isolde's stomach. She'd been correct about his motives. "You'll never get past me to get to her," Isolde said with as much bravado as she could. Her injured arm was aching and she felt her energy fade as her earlier battles took their toll.

Drawing on everything she had inside her, Isolde held her sword in her right hand and gripped her *sgian-dubh* in her left, then waited for the lieutenant to attack. When he did, she met his stroke and blocked it. He came at her again with a powerful arc of his blade. Isolde feinted to the left and slashed the lieutenant's thigh with her blade, drawing blood.

The lieutenant did not cry out in pain, but his eyes flared with fury. He slashed at Isolde over and over again like an injured animal no longer able to contain his savagery, willing to sacrifice all for the sake of cutting her down.

Isolde's heart pounded in her ears as fear crept past her guard. The man was erratic, making it almost impossible to predict his moves. If she were going to walk away from this conflict, she needed to do something and fast. Tapping into reserves of strength she didn't know she possessed, Isolde advanced.

The lieutenant's eyes widened in surprise. Their blades

came together with such force that sparks flared. The two swords locked together at the hilt. Isolde wrenched the sword from Lieutenant Collins's grasp, sending it arcing wildly across the courtyard and onto the packed earth.

The motion set her opponent off balance and he fell to the ground several yards away from his sword. He stared at his weapon in shocked disbelief.

Isolde used his momentary distraction to finish the deed as she poised her blade at the soft tissue of the lieutenant's neck. If he moved, the sharp edge of her blade would end his life. "Do you yield?"

Lieutenant Collins remained silent as his chest rose and fell with the force of his breathing. "Aye," he finally replied.

At the lieutenant's words, the fighting in the courtyard stopped. "Do you swear that you will leave here and never return? Or send other troops to battle for you?"

The lieutenant's gaze turned mutinous. "Very soon, not even the MacLeods can avoid what is coming."

Isolde pressed her sword more firmly against his throat, drawing blood. "Your word, Lieutenant. Swear you will not return."

"I promise never to return to Dunvegan," he spat out.

"And?"

The lieutenant's gaze hardened. "I will not send any further men to battle the MacLeods."

Isolde lifted her sword and the lieutenant twisted away. He staggered to his feet, gathered his sword, and limped towards the gates with his men behind him.

Isolde waited and watched until the last man was over the drawbridge. Only when the iron portcullis closed behind the enemy did she finally lower her bloodied sword. The battle was over.

Gwendolyn and Rowena entered the courtyard with Fiona and Emlyn following behind. Isolde drew an easier breath knowing the women and the young girl were unharmed. The English had not succeeded with their plan to force Alastair and all of the MacLeods to stand with the English against their countrymen.

"Are you well?" Gwendolyn asked when she reached Isolde's side. Slowly, the tension that had driven her during the battle drained away, leaving only exhaustion and pain.

"We must see to the wounded and bury the dead," Isolde said.

Gwendolyn stayed her with a touch to her arm. "You have done enough for us this day. I insist you go inside and let us take care of you now."

"She'll need a bath and a new dress," Fiona stated with a sympathetic look at her soiled clothing. "And no doubt a visit from Lottie to resew the wound at your arm. It appears to have reopened while you were fighting."

Isolde looked down at her arm to see blood dripping from the bottom part of her partially healed wound. She had pushed herself to the limits today but had ultimately overcome the enemy with the help of the castle guards and the mysterious woman who had appeared on the tower. Could she have had something to do with opening the gates? What was it the Grey Lady had said? 'Someone will unknowingly betray the clan.' Or was the woman with the white hair an image Isolde had conjured up in a time of great need? She should keep her suspicions to herself until she could prove the woman had been real.

"Isolde? Are you all right?" Isolde's thoughts were broken by Gwendolyn touching her arm.

"I'm well enough," Isolde replied, bringing her thoughts back to the moment. "My wound is nothing when compared to the injuries others have no doubt sustained. Lottie must care for them first."

Gwendolyn shook her head. "Nay. I insist you let us care for you first. If not for you, those men who entered the castle would have reached me and the outcome of this battle would be entirely different."

"Agreed." Rowena's gaze said she would not take no for an answer either. "Once you and the injured are seen to, I will also try to determine who opened the castle gates."

Gwendolyn's face paled. "I fear we have yet another traitor amongst us."

Rowena offered Gwendolyn a sympathetic look. "We'll find them. We always do."

Oblivious to the seriousness of the conversation going on around her, Emlyn bent to retrieve the *sgian-dubh* Isolde had dropped and held it out before her. "I want to be a warrior just like you." The young girl did her best to imitate Isolde, swinging her sword in front of her.

Isolde looked about her and moved to pick up a small stick that would have been the size of a small sword. She took her blade from the girl's hands and offered her the stick. "You should practise with this first until I can make you a proper wooden sword."

"You'll make me a sword?" Emlyn swung her makeshift weapon left then right, demonstrating her skill. "I want to protect people like you do."

Isolde couldn't help but smile. The girl reminded her of herself at that age. "I will agree to letting Lottie sew my arm, a bath, and new garments." Her gaze swung to Rowena and the interesting clothing she wore. "Are those breeches you are wearing or armour?"

Rowena smiled. "A little of both. This outfit was made for one of our ancestors for battling our enemies. I've decided to put it to use again." Growing more serious, she added, "It's imbued with fairy magic to help protect the one wearing it."

Isolde's eyes went wide. "Perhaps you should have more made for all the MacLeods."

"That is not a poor idea," Rowena said quirking her brow. "I'll have to talk to Mother about that."

"Could I make a request about those new garments?" Isolde hesitated, then said, "Could I ask for a tunic and a pair of breeches for myself?"

"After what you did to save us," Gwendolyn replied, "we will give you whatever you desire."

Isolde instantly sobered. No one could give her what she truly wanted. Not now that Lieutenant Collins knew where she was and that she still lived. Nowhere and no one in Scotland would be safe around her. For while she'd managed to get the Englishman to declare he wouldn't harm the MacLeods; she'd forced no such promise upon him for herself.

As soon as Lottie sewed her arm, after she bathed and changed, then made a wooden sword for Emlyn, she would leave.

<hr />

ARIA WAITED IN the bedchamber where she'd been hiding, waiting for silence to settle over the castle, wrestling with her own demons. What had she done to the MacLeods today by opening the gates? She had wanted to see how the strong and independent women she'd watched for days would respond to a male visitor. Aria had had no idea that man in the red uniform was their enemy.

As soon as conflict had broken out, Aria had grabbed her bow and quiver and raced to the tower to help. Now all that exertion had taken its toll. She was hungry. Nay, she was famished. She usually waited until the family was in the great hall during a meal or in bed for the night to walk the halls, exploring. Her growling stomach objected to that idea.

Once it was quiet, she would sneak down to the kitchen and help herself to whatever she could find. After her hunger settled, she would determine what to do next. The woman they called Izzy had seen her on the tower. Aria's presence was no longer a secret. It would be best if she presented herself and her offer sooner rather than later. Perhaps when the MacLeod men returned.

A bedchamber door closed farther down the hallway. Aria silently opened the door and peered out to see Gwendolyn and Rowena heading for the staircase. She closed the door and turned back to the chamber. Only a few moments more and she could search for food.

The bedchamber she'd been hiding in had a layer of dust on every surface, as though it hadn't been used in a very long time. White sheets had covered the furnishings when she'd first entered the chamber. She had since stripped them from the bed and a chest of drawers so that she could use them.

On the top of the chest of drawers she'd found a brush and comb that she'd put to use, as well as a small miniature of a woman with dark hair and soulful grey eyes. The woman looked very much like Rowena, except years older. Her mother perhaps?

Aria's own mother's hair had been red, her skin fair, and she'd had eyes that were as blue as the sea on a summer's day, which made sense since her mother's magic could control water and all manner of water fairies and selkies. As a half-fae

Aria only had magic over freshwater brooks and rivers, but nothing to do with the sea or saltwater.

Aria continued her appraisal of the bedchamber while she waited for those who were still about to settle. She'd yet to find a likeness of her father. Perhaps there were none, and she'd always be left to wonder what kind of man abandoned his own child. Or, had it been her mother who had failed her by returning to Fairyland before she'd been born where she'd been forced to live in a world where she only half-belonged?

Leaving her thoughts behind, Aria opened the door and peered into the hallway once more. This time the corridor was empty. Her stomach gave another growl of protest as she stepped outside the bedchamber and silently crept to the stairs. She had successfully made her way to the second floor, when an unearthly chill came over her and a mist curled across the floor, swirling and consolidating until something not quite human and not quite ghost appeared in front of her.

Why are you here?

Aria's heart leapt in her chest at the sight of the woman from the miniature in her borrowed bedchamber. "Who are you?" The woman's piercing grey eyes raked her, assessed her. The ghost's gaze narrowed on her face, and a flash of recognition flared, then vanished.

Are you here to harm my children? I will never allow that.

Aria bristled. "I helped them today. I did not harm

them."

You were the one who invited the enemy inside these walls.

"I did not know what would happen. From my observations, it appeared to me as if the MacLeods have led ideal lives. Who would have guessed they would have so many enemies?" She'd always imagined the MacLeods as invincible.

You think my children have led ideal lives, that they are invincible? In that you couldn't be more wrong. All of us have suffered in some way because we are MacLeods.

"You can hear my thoughts?" Aria frowned. She would have to be more careful in the future. She straightened as her stomach grumbled again. A ghost wasn't going to stop her from her quest for food. With a quick intake of breath, Aria stepped right through the image of the woman before her and continued down the stairs. And then froze in her tracks.

The ghost's icy form enveloped her. She tried to take a step, but found she could not. "What do you want from me?"

I want you to leave this place. I know who you are, Aria. You were here once before when you came to Dunvegan with your mother.

Aria swallowed to ease the tightness in her throat. "How could you know that?"

An anxious frown formed a wrinkle between the woman's other-worldly brows. *I was a mortal woman then, known to you and your mother as Janet MacLeod. I tried to help you, but my efforts instead led to my own death and the disappear-*

ance of my son, Keiran. Would you know anything about that?

Her voice was almost inaudible, but it caused fear to cascade through Aria, making her light-headed. This was the child's mother? "That is why I am here—to tell your kin about Keiran."

The apparition held ominously still as grief distorted her features. *Tell me, is he still alive?*

"He is. Though my grandfather used magic on him to accelerate his age. He is now twenty in human years."

The apparition staggered back, releasing Aria from her frozen prison. *For years I have wondered . . . I wanted to search for him, but I was trapped here in this form.*

"You cannot leave Dunvegan?"

Nay. But you must. Her voice was vibrant with urgency. *You must leave or swear to me you will cause my family no further harm. We have suffered enough already because of you.*

Aria felt a cold chill ripple down her spine. "I mean your children no harm, I promise."

The apparition's shoulders sagged as though relieved by her answer. *Is there a way to bring him home?*

"There is a way. That is what I have come to discuss with your sons."

Then why are you hiding in the bedchamber?

"I needed time to consider how to tell them. I also wanted to make certain they would believe me. And I needed to measure their nature to see if they would accept me as their kin."

The daughter of Iain Cair.

"The child your husband, the laird, refused to take in," Aria said bitterly as the memories flooded back.

Sympathy reflected in the woman's soulful eyes. *My husband used to be a gentle man but he changed. He became brutal and suspicious after he sustained an injury to his head in battle. Had you and your mother arrived a few months earlier the outcome might have been different for both of us.*

Aria's stomach growled and then twisted at the knowledge. For the first time ever, she sympathised with Norman MacLeod. The two sides of her heritage had been at war with each other for years. The human side longed for kinship. The fairy side demanded mischief. Which side would win her over on any given day was always a mystery, even to her. Perhaps it was much the same for him after his injury.

Aria frowned as she remembered what else the ghost had said. "What do you mean? How was anything different for you?"

The woman dropped her gaze. *As a result of helping you and your mother escape, the laird took his anger out on me and threw me into the dungeon. I died there, and yet I stayed at Dunvegan as a ghost.*

Aria gasped. "You are a ghost because of me?"

I know not why I am as I am. Perhaps I will never know. You, however, have a chance to know your kin now. Do not let that opportunity pass you by.

"What if they won't accept me?"

I accept you and thank you for helping in the earlier battle. Isolde will accept you as well. She saw you on the tower. She knows what you have done to help the MacLeods this day and will advocate for you, if you will allow it.

"Truly?"

The ghost nodded.

"I want more than anything to belong here at Dunvegan."

In order for that to happen, you must talk to Alastair and his brothers. Tell them who you are and that their brother, Keiran, still lives.

"I shall do that when the proper time presents itself. With the men away, now is not the moment." Deep in thought, Aria moved down the stairway to the first floor and opened the door to the outside. Her gaze fixed in the distance beyond the castle gates and the rugged landscape beyond. "I long to stay here as I am in awe of this world and its breathtaking scenery. Fairyland is so different." Her words were only a thread above a whisper. "I do not believe I have ever seen anything more beautiful than Dunvegan and the land surrounding it."

Dunvegan is a haven of peace in a land that has chosen to go to war with itself.

Aria's stomach grumbled, loudly.

The apparition gazed down at Aria. *If you are hungry, I would gladly accompany you to the kitchen. The MacLeods share what they have with those in need.*

"I would like that." Aria couldn't hold back a smile. She

was talking to her first MacLeod since her arrival. It didn't matter that the woman was a ghost. It was the start of something she'd longed for her whole life.

CHAPTER TWELVE

T HE LATE-MORNING MIST left a chill in the air that only
amplified the tension emanating from the MacLeod
warriors as they finally reached the edge of the village of
Roag. Spirals of smoke rose into the sky from four buildings.
Orrick's stomach roiled at the scent of burning wood. For a
moment, he was back in a small village in the West Indies
that had been devastated by the English. They'd set torches
to everything and killed everyone—man, woman, and child.

Orrick shook off the memory. Whoever had attacked
Roag had already left. For that small blessing Orrick was
grateful. Despite Alastair's claim that Orrick was ready for
battle, he wasn't so certain.

Riding into the centre of the village, Orrick stopped and
dismounted near a group of men. They appeared shaken as
they talked about the men who had burned their church, two
cottages on the outskirts of the village, and the guildhall on
the edge of the market. All the buildings had been empty at
the time. And no one had been killed or injured.

"No one was killed in the attack?" Orrick asked, growing
suspicious of who the attackers were.

A bearded older man shook his head. "'Twas the strangest thing. 'Twas as if the riders were only here tae scare us."

Alastair and Tormod joined Orrick, both of his brothers shooting a dark frown at the older man. "Did you recognise any of the attackers?" Alastair asked.

"Nay," the man replied and the others near him shook their heads.

Tormod's fists were curled. "Were they wearing clan colours?"

"Nae that we could see. They were all dressed in hooded black capes," another man said.

"How many of them were there?" Orrick's sense that something wasn't quite right intensified.

"Only ten." The youngest of the men crossed his arms over his chest and scowled. "We could've fought back 'cuz our numbers are greater. But they came and left so quickly, we only had time tae grab our weapons before they were gone."

Orrick's gut tightened as he exchanged a look with his brothers. "This attack doesn't follow the pattern of the one that devastated Orbost last week."

Alastair's features darkened. "Probably because it wasn't the MacQueens or even the MacDonalds who attacked."

"Then who attacked?" Tormod asked.

Orrick's gaze clashed with Alastair's as they both said, "The English."

Tormod flexed his hands as though in preparation for a

battle. "Which direction did they head?"

"I saw them headin' tae the north," the older man said.

"Should we pursue them?" the younger man asked, his body tensing.

"Nay," Alastair replied. "You are needed here to help be sure the fires are doused, and make certain everyone truly is unharmed. My men and I will go after them."

Orrick's gaze moved about the village and the people who, seeing the MacLeods were no threat, emerged from their homes. Orrick's thoughts were scattered as he tried to piece together this puzzle. Why attack a village and leave minimal damage? What purpose would something like that serve?

A moment later, a fist of fear closed around Orrick's heart, making it difficult to breathe. "God's bones!" he exclaimed, not liking the progression of his thoughts. "We took most of the warriors with us, leaving Dunvegan with only a few well-trained men to protect the castle and those inside." He swallowed roughly. "What if this attack was only meant to lead us away so that Lieutenant Collins's regiment could attack there?" Orrick's gaze shifted to Alastair. Could his brother have made a huge tactical error by bringing all three brothers here to this village? Alastair never made such mistakes, at least not in the past.

"What would he be after?" Alastair asked with a furrowed brow.

"The women," Orrick said, clenching his fists at his

sides. "If Collins captures Gwendolyn or Fiona, he could force you or Tormod to declare your support of the English king with very little effort on his part." Orrick was surprised he was the one to consider that possibility. His mind had been foggy since returning from the West Indies; he'd thought himself no longer capable of strategic or defensive thoughts.

"If that is the case, we can't be in two places at once." Tormod's voice was hard, stressed.

"We can, if we divide the men," Alastair said. "We can send half to follow those who attacked here, and the other half back to Dunvegan."

"The fires are under control, and only a few men are needed tae see that they are fully extinguished. We have horses and men who can help you go after those who attacked us," the older man beside them offered.

Alastair nodded. "We would be thankful for any assistance. How soon can you be ready?"

"Not long. We only have tae gather horses," the youngest of the village men said.

Alastair nodded once more. "We will meet you at the edge of town in a few minutes."

The men hurried away.

Tormod's features steeled as his gaze passed between Orrick and Alastair. "If you two promise to ride like the wind, I will lead the men in pursuit of the English who attacked here."

"We'll not let any harm come to Fiona," Alastair assured Tormod as he swung up onto his horse's back. "God be with you, Brother."

"And with you," Tormod echoed as he mounted and headed towards the MacLeod warriors to divide them.

Orrick strode to his horse and swung up into the saddle. He and Alastair waited for the warriors to fall in behind them after Tormod divided them. Not only were Gwendolyn, Fiona, and Rowena at risk back at Dunvegan, Isolde was there as well, and still incapacitated by her wound. If the English attacked, would she be able to at least defend the women with her sword?

If Lieutenant Collins learned of her presence at the castle, what would he do to her? At the thought of losing her to the Englishman or anyone else, an empty ache came to his chest. Isolde was different. Special. She was unlike any other woman he had ever met. She, more than anyone else, understood the painful memories he'd brought back with him from the West Indies.

He and Isolde were kindred spirits whether she wanted to admit it or not. Orrick smiled wistfully at the memory of their first meeting when he came face to face with not only her arrow but also the beautiful creature holding a bow.

That smile slipped a moment later when the men were ready, and he and Alastair turned their horses back down the path they had travelled only a short while ago. Orrick encouraged his horse into a faster gait as he scanned the landscape for signs of the English. Alastair increased his speed as well, seeming as desperate to get home as Orrick was.

The sun was high in the sky when the four-storey fortress of golden-brown stones came into view. With a hungry gaze, Orrick searched the courtyard as they approached, looking for a glimpse of Isolde. He caught no sight of her golden hair, or any guards, for that matter. The towers of the castle appeared deserted and ribbons of smoke coiled high into the air above the castle.

Alastair's alarmed gaze connected with his. "Something has happened here," Alastair said, kicking his horse into a full gallop. "Open the gates!"

The thunder of hoofbeats matched the pounding of Orrick's heart as the gate slowly started to rise, revealing several dead Englishmen lying in the courtyard.

"There appears to have been a battle." The gate seemed to take forever to rise due to his impatience.

Alastair must have had the same thought that the gate was slow to open. As he jumped down from his horse, Orrick followed and they both bent to slide under the partially open portcullis, then raced into the courtyard.

Everywhere there was silence. Orrick's heart seemed to freeze as he ran faster past men who were slain by a sword. Without thinking what he was doing, he drew his weapon.

"Gwendolyn!" Alastair's exclamation was part summoning, part battle cry.

When they reached the door to the castle, they threw it open and skidded to a halt inside the foyer to see more Englishmen lying dead at the bottom of the stairs and all the way up to the first floor.

Orrick's heart moved to his throat. "We're too late." It was then he noticed the arrows protruding from the dead men's chests. Not MacLeod men. *Had Isolde defended the castle in their absence?*

"Everyone is down at the loch," a familiar male voice came from behind them.

Orrick spun around to see Becks, the steward. His clothing was smeared with blood and dirt.

"Explain this," Alastair demanded.

"The English waited until you and your brothers had left, then someone inside our castle opened the gates and let them in. The English attacked the guards, then once past them, they tried to kidnap Gwendolyn."

Alastair paled. "Where is my wife?"

"She is safe. Gwendolyn, Fiona, and Rowena are burning the bodies of the dead at the shoreline since the English left their dead behind."

Alastair rushed to the back doorway and out into the rear courtyard. He did not stop until he stood at the balustrade overlooking the shoreline. Below Fiona and Rowena stood near the burning pyres while Gwendolyn distributed blankets to the castle staff who were chilled from the wind along the shoreline. At the sight of his wife, Alastair released an audible breath. "Were any of our warriors killed or injured?" he asked Becks when the steward and Orrick appeared at Alastair's side.

"Lottie is with the four men who were injured. No one was killed."

"And Izzy?" Orrick asked, searching the shoreline.

A deep sorrow weighed down Beck's appearance, making him look older and more tired than he'd ever looked before.

"Tell me, I beg you."

"She left before any of us knew she was gone."

Orrick's breath stilled in his chest. "Gone? Why?"

"She left a note for Gwendolyn and Alastair. She also left a note in her chamber for you, Orrick, along with a wooden sword for Emlyn." Becks extended his hand back towards the doorway. "Izzy protected the womenfolk who were upstairs at the time of the attack. If it weren't for her bravery and skill, I fear Gwendolyn might have been captured, and who knows what else might have happened."

Shame weighed Orrick down. Isolde had done what he could not. Obviously, Isolde's aim had improved under the weight of the challenge before her. Without her this day might have become a tragedy. And yet, she'd still felt as though she didn't belong here with the MacLeods. If anyone didn't belong here, it was Orrick. He was a MacLeod. He had at one time been a mighty warrior. What would it take to become that man again? To be more like Isolde?

"Orrick?"

Orrick shook his head, dispelling his thoughts and found Alastair staring at him with concern.

"Where did you go?"

Orrick glanced at Alastair, then noted that Becks had left, most likely to allow the men to talk in private. "I do not want to be the man who cannot do what must be done to protect his family. I don't want to disappoint you or anyone else by not being able to battle as I should. I always retreated into my books when I felt unworthy as a child and then as a young man. It is why I tossed those books aside and went to the West Indies with Tormod. I was trying to prove to myself that I could be just like the two of you."

Alastair frowned. "We never wanted you to be anything but what you already are. You give the three of us balance. I stop and plan, Tormod rushes to fight without thinking, but you—you were always the perfect mixture of both. You gave every situation great thought, but then you were prepared for whatever came our way—from the surrounding terrain, to our enemies' strengths and weaknesses, to the types of weaponry or strategy that would be most effective while sparing lives whenever we did have to battle." Alastair placed a hand on Orrick's arm. "Tormod and I always wanted to be more like you."

Orrick gaped at his brother, amazed. "Truly?"

Alastair nodded. "I'm sorry I pushed you earlier to fight with Tormod and me. I won't do that again. When you are ready—" Alastair shrugged "—if you are ever ready, then I will gladly have you ride beside me into battle."

"Thank you, Brother." Orrick managed a smile. Talking with Alastair had helped ease the shame he'd felt earlier. "You should go be with Gwendolyn."

"And you should go find Isolde and bring her back here, where she belongs. We all owe her a debt of gratitude for what she has done this day."

Orrick pushed his fingers through his hair, suddenly feeling restless. More than anything he wanted to find Isolde and bring her home. Dunvegan no longer felt right without her. "I think I know where to find her."

"Do you want me to go with you?" Alastair asked.

"You are needed here. Besides, I am certain you are anxious to see Gwendolyn. Perhaps I could take Graeme with me and a few men."

Alastair nodded. "As soon as I see Gwendolyn, I will make it so."

CHAPTER THIRTEEN

I SOLDE WAITED AND watched from her hiding place amongst the brambles and tall grasses that were within spying distance from her cave. She had to make certain no one was around before she went back to gather what meagre supplies remained there. She would also bring her bed, the few dishes she'd carved out of wood, and her stash of arrows to the secondary cave she had started at the base of Healabhal Mór.

As she waited, she saw red deer passing through the tall grass, munching on the blades that were dusted with snow. She'd left before Lottie had come to sew her wound and before anyone could stop her. She still wore her battered and bloody dress from earlier in the day, the boots they'd provided her, and the wool cloak Orrick had placed around her shoulders. The boots were a true luxury after a year of wearing shoes she'd fashioned for herself, but the cloak wasn't nearly as warm as the pelted one she'd left behind. She'd have to remedy that by creating a new one or she might perish from the winter weather.

Along with the deer, a badger family passed by: a mother

and three cubs that had been born earlier that year. For a moment, the mother stopped and sniffed the air, possibly smelling the blood on her clothing or sensing Isolde's nearness. The badger reared up on her hind legs, searching the grass with her cubs behind her.

Isolde tensed. The badger was protecting her cubs from an unseen threat. Then, as though sensing Isolde was not a threat, the animal lowered her wedge-shaped body back onto four paws and continued leading her family to a safer location. Isolde watched them head away from her, then turned to gaze down at her injured arm. The animal world was no different than the human world. They would do whatever they had to in order to protect what was precious to them.

Isolde sobered. She had protected what was treasured at Dunvegan, then had fled in order to stop putting them in danger. Would they see her sacrifice as such or would they think her a coward for leaving? Would Orrick come looking for her? She knew she shouldn't want him to, but she couldn't stop thinking about him and the passionate kiss they'd shared. She closed her eyes and swallowed, clenching her fists. That kiss had left her shaken and confused, and longing for more of what she could never have.

Her stomach clenched, and she felt a sudden ache where her heart was. Isolde opened her eyes and pushed the sensation away. Leaving Orrick behind was what she had to do to keep him and his clan safe, no matter how much she longed for a different outcome.

She regretted not staying long enough to find the woman with the white hair who had helped her in the battle against Lieutenant Collins and his men. She'd mentioned the woman in her letter to Alastair and Gwendolyn. It was up to them to decide how to proceed on that front.

The sun was starting to set, casting the world around Isolde in hues of grey and gold. She would only have daylight for perhaps an hour, or less. If she were going to make it to Healabhal Mór tonight, she would have to travel by moonlight.

She cast one final glance around the area leading up to the cave and determined that she was indeed alone. But just in case someone waited inside the cave, she strung her bow and proceeded to the entrance.

When Isolde reached the mouth of the cave, she stepped inside and listened. Her previous home was dark and silent. She made not a sound as she stepped farther into the darkness, feeling emptiness grow inside her. She'd been with the MacLeods for a week, but now her old home felt cold and dreary, hostile and unforgiving.

With the flint and steel she'd left behind in the cave, she lit the remnants of a candle she'd taken from the MacLeods, then set the flame to the torch at the midway point of her cave. As soon as the light flared, she dropped the candle and clutched her bow, ready to draw an arrow in case someone or something was there.

The cave was empty. She should have been grateful; instead she felt even more alone. A lump lodged in her throat. It would take some time to get used to the solitude of living on her own again, relying only on herself for her survival.

Relaxing her bow, Isolde walked over to her bed where she had placed Emlyn after she'd sewn the child's leg, then to the shelf where Orrick had retrieved her gathered honey. Isolde still felt their presence. They'd only been in her life for little more than a week, but she could not deny the fact that she missed them both terribly. Her heart clenched and a chill settled inside her, spreading through her limbs.

"I am not lonely," she said aloud, the sound echoing in the cave. If she kept telling herself that lie, then perhaps someday it might be the truth. She used to think her world outside Scorrybreac was expansive. She had no walls to hold her captive. She could go anywhere and do anything without the disapproval of her brother. Although, she did regret not being amongst her people. That was why she'd trained so hard all her life: To protect them. And not just those behind the walls of Scorrybreac: all the Scottish people.

When her father and mother had returned from their travels with glorious tales, she'd had a glimpse of a wondrous world full of many peoples and cultures. She'd also been given insight into what larger problems might come their way with British expansion. England was Scotland's neighbour. Scotland had already lost her independence when King James I had become the heir to the English throne. Now they might very well lose their national identity if they didn't keep fighting. It would take every well-trained warrior to see that didn't happen. Including Isolde.

Once she reached her new home, she would figure out how to make that happen even if it meant fighting by herself. She gathered her honey pot, her bowl and cup, and placed them on the pelt covering her bed before gathering the pile of arrows she'd fletched herself over the past year. She had tied the items into a bundle when she heard the snap of a branch just outside the cave. Her muscles tensed. She dropped the pelt and drew an arrow from her quiver, setting it to her bow. She spun towards the opening with her heart in her throat.

In the purple light of dusk she saw the familiar outline of Orrick's body. When he stepped into the light, she eased the arrow from her bow. This morning his eyes had been filled with warmth and acceptance. Now they were filled with uncertainty.

"Why did you leave Dunvegan?" he asked, his gaze dropping to the bundled pelt at her feet.

"You should not have come," she said even as warmth centred in her chest at the sight of him.

"I had to. You matter to me, Isolde. I needed to know you were safe." Orrick's gaze shifted to her injured arm as he stepped closer.

"My arm is fine, as is my aim once more. You no doubt saw evidence of that upon your return to Dunvegan." Isolde glanced at the entrance of the cave. Had Orrick come alone?

"Graeme and seven others are waiting for us at a distance. I asked for privacy while we talked," he said as though reading the directions of her thoughts.

Now others knew about her secluded home. It was now more important than ever that she leave for her secondary settlement and soon—darkness was falling.

"We can talk here or back at the castle, but we will talk. The choice is up to you," Orrick said, interrupting her thoughts.

He stood before her. She doubted the trick she'd used to slip past him the first time would be successful again. So she stepped back and sat on the man-made ledge carved out of the stone wall.

He took a seat at the rough table opposite her. They sat in silence. She was about to break the moment when he sighed. "We are friends, are we not?"

Her brows came together. "Aye."

"Then why leave Dunvegan and the protection we offer you?" He looked away, then back at her. "I need an honest answer."

"I have always been honest with you." A trickle of discomfort crept down Isolde's spine. "I wasn't certain I was welcome by anyone but you, and the other women. If the laird does not approve of me, life at Dunvegan could be almost as bad for me as it is on my own out here."

"Alastair's feelings for you have changed since we were

lured away from the castle so that the English could strike. My brother is grateful that you protected his wife, our sister, and all the members of our household. Without you, who knows what horrors the English might have unleashed in our absence?"

"I did what I had to do, what I was trained to do," she said softly because the lump in her throat was so large. "Earlier today, I saw the badger family who mauled me and Emlyn. It was a mother and her three cubs, and suddenly I understood why she attacked us. She saw us as a threat and protected her young. Just as I protected the females of your clan. Just as your mother protects you and your siblings by remaining with you as a ghost."

He nodded his understanding as she continued. "I'm not certain it was the right thing to do, but I allowed the leader of the English soldiers to leave Dunvegan. I did make him promise never to return."

"I would like to hear more about how you wrested that promise from our enemy, but you still haven't answered my question. Why did you leave . . . me?" Orrick's voice faded as he regarded her, his brow furrowing. "Meeting you was one of the best things that has ever happened to me. I hadn't realised until we met how heavy my spirit had been for so many years. In your presence, I felt renewed, lightened, hopeful."

Knowing she should keep her distance yet unable to do so, she knelt before him and took his chilled hands in hers.

"Before I answer your question, can I ask you something that might be difficult?"

His lips pulled up in a momentary smile. "Seems only fair."

"You mentioned your spirit being heavy. I assume you are talking about your time in the West Indies."

He nodded.

"Could the memories that refuse to leave you in peace . . . could they be because instead of fighting to protect those you loved, you were paid to battle?"

He frowned. "I'd never considered such a thing." There was enough light from the torch she'd lit to see the swift procession of emotions that crossed his features: disbelief, confusion, then horror. "You might be right. I had never had nightmares when protecting my people before the West Indies." He frowned. "Why did I fail to protect you from danger in the wilderness when we first met if that is the case? That I didn't recognise you at first is no excuse. You were in need. I should have helped you."

"You were out of practise." She offered him a smile. "That has changed." She hadn't realised how tense she'd become until she started to relax.

He returned a half-smile. "Thank you for accepting me and all my faults."

"We all have faults, Orrick. Your hesitation to fight others is not a weakness. It shows how much inner strength you have to stop and think about what you are doing, and why.

It must have been so difficult for you growing up in the shadow of two older brothers who always seem so confident and sure of themselves. You survived the West Indies and all the challenges there. And you've proven to me in the past week you can overcome any obstacle that has risen before you."

"Not every obstacle," he said in a warm, almost seductive tone.

Her gaze connected with his and her breath stilled at the warm, sensual look that now filled his brown eyes.

"Now it's your turn to answer my question." His gaze held hers.

She swallowed roughly. He'd asked for the truth. She looked away, then back at him again. "I left because I was scared. Hiding from everyone and even myself is all I've done for the past year. I didn't want to put you or your family at further risk by my presence at Dunvegan. Even though I made Lieutenant Collins promise to leave the MacLeods in peace, I have no idea if he truly will."

"The MacLeods are capable of taking care of their own when all of us are in residence. We will not fall for such a trick as we did again." Orrick smiled. "Besides, with you on our side, we would definitely have an advantage over any enemy who chose to strike." His smile faded as he studied her face. "Will you leave this cave behind you and come home with me?" She pressed her lips together. Part of her wanted to go back with him, yet part of her was still uncertain. He might think he could protect his people from the English, but she'd seen first-hand what their neighbours to the south were capable of. The Scots were ill-prepared for a full English invasion.

Sensing her confusion, Orrick reached out and stroked her cheek with his thumb. "It's late and darkness has fallen. We should stay here tonight, and then in the morning you can decide to leave or return to Dunvegan with me."

A spiral of longing moved through her at his intimate touch. "What about Graeme and the others who came with you?"

"They are prepared to set up camp if I do not rejoin them right away."

"What if the English come during the night?"

His thumb outlined the fullness of her bottom lip. "Do they know about your cave?"

"Nay. Only you, and now Graeme and the others." She breathed in the scent of the earth that permeated the cooling air of the evening.

Orrick stepped closer and held out his hand. "Isolde."

She released a deep shuddering breath. He'd called her by her true name, not the name "Izzy" they had forced upon her. She could feel the warmth of him against her chest, yet they did not touch. He lifted the end of her plait where it hung across her shoulder and curled it round his finger. Slowly, he drew her forward until her hips touched his.

He toyed with the ribbon at the end of her plait until it

fell to the floor. With gentle pressure he worked his thumb and forefinger back and forth. Loosening the weave plait by plait, drawing her closer with each stroke of his finger and thumb. "Your hair is as soft as spun silk." Desire deepened his tone.

At the sound, a shiver moved through her. Her breasts brushed his chest as he brought the fall of her unbound hair up to his mouth. He brushed her hair against his lips then let it fall back against her neck and shoulders. His lips followed her hair down. He pressed the softest of kisses to her hair and the flesh beneath.

She shuddered at the contact. "Orrick, we should not pursue anything further between us. 'Tis too dangerous."

"Everything in my head agrees with you, but having you in my arms feels right."

Unable to stop herself, she pulled him closer and he buried his face in her hair. She felt the strength of his body against hers, could feel the beat of his heart against her chest, and the longing she'd tried to keep at bay swamped her. Since she'd escaped the English, she'd been alone, had wanted to be alone, until he had come along.

He held her tighter. "Tell me if you want to stop."

Isolde felt Orrick's body tighten. He bade her to tell him to stop even as his lips once again found her neck, the sensitive curl of her shoulder, the base of her throat. She meant to tell him to stop as he pushed the edges of her cloak aside then trailed his fingers over her arm and her thigh, gently caressing the hidden flesh beneath her dress. She meant to stop him as he traced lines of hot delight down her chin, across the rise of her breasts.

So much was at stake if they continued. Not only her heart and her virginity, but he might get her with child. Then she would be out in the wilderness trying to take care of herself and an innocent child. His relationship with his clan was also at risk. He'd said Alastair had changed his opinion of her, but many others still had not.

She forced back a groan of equal parts despair and desire as Orrick's lips covered hers. His tongue teased the seam of her lips. If they continued, they would forge a bond between the MacLeod and Nicolson clans that would forever put them in conflict with her brother. John was not one to easily forgive her past mistakes.

Even those things did not pull her back. She didn't want to stop him. She didn't want to stop herself. On a groan of capitulation, she leaned into his kiss, opened her lips, and he delved in, igniting a flame that could no longer be quenched.

His fingers found the clasp of her cloak and released it, sending the garment to the ground before moving to the ties of her gown. A heartbeat later, her dress fell to her ankles and she stood before him in only her chemise.

Despite her state of undress, she had never been warmer. The heat came from within her in unquenchable waves of desire. She removed his cloak and the muslin shirt beneath. Her fingers stalled on the laces of his breeches.

"Allow me." His fingers quickly unfastened his breeches. His boots followed. "Take off your chemise," he said in ragged tones. "I don't trust myself not to tear it from you."

His words delighted and terrified. She stared at him uncertainly. He looked fierce, almost tormented.

"Hurry." He stripped off his braies and tossed them to the ground, his gaze never leaving her face. "No second thoughts." He stood naked before her. Starkly, boldly aroused. "I couldn't take it if you had regrets now."

She stared at the man before her. Thick brown hair covered his chest. She followed the V downward, across his flat abdomen, to the silvery wounds that laced his torso, to the thick nest of hair surrounding his rampant arousal. Isolde swallowed and moistened her lips. She should have reservations about what was to come, but she didn't. It felt right being here with Orrick like this—completely and utterly right. "No second thoughts."

He reached for her, pulling her tight against his bare flesh. Her naked breasts pressed against the coarse hair of his chest. The sensation was strangely seductive against the smoothness of her flesh.

He held her close and pressed a gentle kiss to the shoulder of her injured arm. "Before I left, Lottie told me she was on her way to sew your wound again, but found you gone. Does reinjuring your wound pain you much?"

"Nothing pains me at the moment."

With a chuckle, he bent to kiss her neck as he slid his left hand down her abdomen to the thatch of curls surrounding her womanhood. His lips moved farther down, to the top of her right breast, to her nipple. With his tongue, he circled her breast in smaller and smaller circles until he lathed her nipple in warmth.

Just when she started to adjust to the new sensation, his hand moved lower still. Slowly, he rubbed back and forth against the juncture of her thighs, igniting a strange burning need.

Isolde gasped and tangled her fingers in his hair. She swayed helplessly as sensation after bewildering sensation tore through her.

She brought her hands down to caress the corded muscle of his arms, his back, clinging to him as though he were the only solid thing in her world. He was all iron muscles and brawny power. And in this moment, he was hers.

The thought made her bold as she allowed her fingers to explore. Snippets of sensation flickered through her mind—rigid muscle against her softness, the scent of mint mixed with rose, the beat of his heart as it mingled with her breathlessness. She let her fingers trail over the hard planes of his chest, his abdomen, and farther down until she came to his manhood. Boldly, she ran two fingers along its length. He released a guttural sound and eased back. His smouldering gaze dropped to her lips and Isolde felt her body ignite all over again.

"Before we follow this to its natural end, I need to ask

you something," he said, his voice raw with desire. "I cannot put this off a moment longer because as warriors neither of us knows what tomorrow might bring. Today proved that."

Isolde stepped back and brought her hand up to his chest, atop his racing heart. "What is it?"

His eyes were dark, veiled with passion, yet in them she also saw clarity. "Marry me, Isolde."

CHAPTER FOURTEEN

"MARRY YOU?" ISOLDE nearly choked on the unexpected words. "Why the sudden recklessness?"

"I wish to bind myself to you, Isolde, because together we are stronger. We are better than we are alone." The sincerity of his words reflected in his gaze.

Time suddenly seemed to stand still around them even as her blood surged through her veins as it never had before. "We can be together without marriage."

"I had thought so as well until I kissed you and you kissed me in return. I want more of what we will share tonight, for as long as we have left on this earth."

Isolde stared at him as her breath came fast and shallow. "Binding yourself to me will mean much hardship for the MacLeods if my brother still harbours anger towards me."

He stepped towards her. "We've overcome obstacles before."

She took a step back. "The English will place a bounty on my head after what I did to them at Dunvegan."

Orrick took her hands in his. "You did not make Lieutenant Collins swear to leave you in peace when you made him promise not to return to Dunvegan or attack the MacLeods again."

"It was more important to protect your clan," she said in a voice that was no stronger than a whisper.

"If you become a MacLeod, then that promise also extends to you." Orrick gave her a hopeful smile.

"Will Lieutenant Collins honour his promise?"

"We must hope he is a man of integrity." Orrick's smile faded.

A breathless moment passed and then another as she considered Orrick's proposal. His features were calm, confident, as though believing she could not deny his request. Then, drawn to him by a will stronger than her own, Isolde took the two steps that would bring their bodies together again.

She felt a flare of warmth move through her as Orrick's strong fingers closed around her own. In the space of a heartbeat, all her reservations melted away. The loneliness that had been ever-present in her life since she'd first held a sword and marked herself as different from other women fell away. Orrick wanted her to be his wife, his partner, however long or temporary that might be. Their lives would be joined. The thought brought as much fear as exhilaration.

"If I marry you, I must ask one thing of you," she said as his smiling lips descended towards hers.

After a thorough kiss, he pulled back. "Anything."

"We must go to Scorrybreac and seek my brother's blessing. There was a time in the past when my brother and I were close, despite our differences. I need his approval."

Orrick's brow arched. "His approval is important to you after he exiled you?" he asked, his voice soft, and with no judgement.

She nodded. "Even with the promise by the English to stay away from Dunvegan, our joining will make the English an enemy of the MacLeods. If I have my brother's approval to the marriage and if he forgives me for my past misdeeds, then he and his clan will not abandon the MacLeods in a time of need."

"Then tomorrow we go to Scorrybreac." A smile returned to his lips. "Tonight we have all to ourselves," he whispered against her cheek as he placed the lightest of kisses along her jaw. When his lips touched the corner of hers, she turned her head to receive his kiss.

Warmth pooled in her belly and arousal flared as she drew him more deeply into her mouth. With her free hand, she trailed her fingers down his shoulder, across his back, until she urged him closer against the softness of her body, fitting the evidence of his arousal tightly against her thigh.

He shifted them both along the cave floor towards the bed. At the edge he broke the kiss and stepped back, going to retrieve the bundled pelt she had dropped earlier. Together they unwrapped it and removed the contents, setting them aside before they stretched the thick, sewn pelts across the moss and feathers.

On the opposite side of the bed, the warmth of Orrick's gaze caressed her. "Not only are you a powerful warrior, you are a beautiful woman, Isolde. A rare combination. What a fortunate man am I." In the soft glow of the torchlight, he came around the bed to stand before her.

"I am the lucky one. I thought I would be alone forever."

He pulled her to him and she gasped, then closed her eyes, overcome by the startling sensation of his warm skin against her own. He brushed his lips across hers before he slid his mouth down her neck, across her shoulders, then farther down until he reached her breasts. He nuzzled them slowly for endless moments before his lips closed over her taut nipples—first one, then the other.

She moaned softly as he increased the pressure of his warm and languid caresses, pulling her into a dark, whirling storm of pure desire and need. She tangled her hand in his hair, feeling the thick, cool silk slide through her fingers. Her legs felt weak beneath her as she drew in the heated, minty scent of his skin.

"Orrick," she called, uncertain what it was she asked for, but she knew she longed for more of this dizzying arousal.

His mouth left her breasts, and still she trembled with the vibrant awareness of his body so close to hers. With a physical effort she forced her eyes open and looked at him. What she saw made her heart ache. In the glow of the firelight, his face was hard and dark with passion, and yet there was as much tenderness in his eyes as longing.

A sudden yearning took hold of her, fired her desire and her boldness. She slid her hand over the rigid muscles of his chest, watching as they flexed instinctively in passionate response to her touch. His reaction—heady, earthly, erotic.

She trailed her fingers over his arms, his neck, and shoulders, following each touch with her lips. His skin was like satin, and heat radiated from him, spreading through her, pulling her into a place without thought, without time, where all she knew were the waves of sensation and fire cresting through her body, and the desperate need for more.

And, for the first time in her life, she allowed herself to free her mind from control and caution. She wanted to touch him, to feel the full length of him against her skin, let her desire take her to places she had never imagined.

He lifted her in his arms and settled her on the pelt, then joined her a heartbeat later. Driven by need, she caressed Orrick's back and hips and buttocks, savouring the firmness of his muscles beneath her hands. Each touch, each kiss sent all rational thought further from her mind until she could only feel something wild and primitive building inside her, racing through her veins, seeking an unknown release.

Orrick must have felt it too if the rapid rise and fall of his chest were any indication, but his response was not filled with the same breathless urgency that pulsed through her. Instead, he took his time, brushing her hair away from her neck with agonising tenderness to press kisses along her collarbone, her shoulder, her breasts. With each sweet kiss, the reality of the world faded until there was nothing left but the two of them, the shadows of the cave, and the stillness of the night.

Orrick slid his hands to her waist, holding her captive, a sweet prisoner, as he cradled her body against his own. Nothing had ever felt more right. His hands moved down to cup her buttocks, the roughened texture of his palms flaring against the satiny softness of her flesh. He closed his eyes and breathed deeply into the tumbled mass of her hair, as though savouring her scent.

"With you, I feel whole," he whispered against her hair. "That piece of myself I left back in the West Indies has slid back into place."

The words sank inside her, warmed her. Before she had time to adjust to that flowering sensation, he trailed his fingers along the lean muscle of her thighs, to her inner thigh, and deep inside her core, bringing her passion to new heights of rapture. She gave a soft cry.

He responded with a single savage groan as he rolled her onto her back, eased his hard thighs between her legs and filled her body with promise and heat.

A sharp gasp tore from her throat at the pain that came as quickly as it eased. Only then did Orrick begin to move, slowly at first, then deeper, filling her more fully with each thrust of his hips. The fire that had smouldered like embers in her belly burst into flame. The heat of it filled her, consumed her, as she sought whatever it was he tried to give her. Helplessly, she moved her hips against his.

Isolde felt as if she teetered on the edge of an abyss, filled with sensations too intense to bear in silence. She could hear breathless cries of pleasure she knew must be hers, but she could no more control them than the mounting waves of honeyed fire that tightened her muscles and arched her back.

Heat spiralled inside her, growing stronger and stronger, until all sensation shattered around her, propelling her into oblivion. A groan escaped Orrick. She held on to him, pulling him with her over the edge of forever.

Every inch of her body, every fibre of her being filled with a warmth and pleasure she had never dreamed possible. In his arms she felt not only safe and protected, but also cherished and consumed. Nothing had ever seemed more natural than having Orrick within her, having his hands caress her body, having his lips upon her own.

He collapsed on top of her, his big body not heavy, only comforting as he nestled his head in the crook of her neck. He lay against her, still intimately entwined, his flesh hot, his breathing heavy.

A shudder ran through her. What had just happened between them? She had never experienced anything so powerful, so all-consuming in her life.

Orrick's breathing gradually steadied, slowed. The tension in his face slowly eased until a look of contentment settled over him. He rolled to his side, ending their intimate contact. His hand moved to her breast, cupping it gently as though he weren't ready to release her altogether.

She wasn't ready for the magic of the night to end either. She'd come to the cave expecting to exile herself forever. And then Orrick had arrived, offering her not only protection, but also a lifetime of bliss. 'Twas a dream come true.

At the thought, a heaviness invaded her chest. Past experience had taught her that dreams ended eventually. She forced the heaviness away, nestling closer to Orrick. The dream was hers for the moment and she would hold on as long as she could. She curled against Orrick's side and let sleep take her where it would.

As the first light of dawn crept in through the opening of the cave, Isolde woke to the sensation that someone was watching her again. Easing off the bed, so as not to wake Orrick, she found her clothing and put it on before she found her bow and quiver, then moved towards the opening.

Drawing an arrow from her quiver and setting it to her bow, Isolde stepped outside. Staying hidden behind the trees and the shelter she'd built, she scrutinised the open moorlands. She saw the tents Graeme and his men had set up, but no one yet stirred. When nothing else appeared, she relaxed her hand on the string of her bow. Why did it always feel as if someone or something was close by, yet she was unable to see anything?

She pressed her lips into a thin line as she headed back inside the cave. At least she could be certain the English had not found her. From what she'd learned about them as their captive, they would not hide their presence. Nay, they would strike her down the moment she showed herself.

Inside the cave, she paused, waiting for the silence to fill her mind as it always did when she entered her home. This morning that silence eluded her. Instead she heard the soft sound of Orrick's breathing. A smile came to her lips before it faltered. Would her brother forgive her? If he did, would he disapprove of her marrying a MacLeod? Their clans were allies, and a tightening of that bond could only help the Nicolson clan. Or, would her brother's heart have hardened against her permanently? Would he take his revenge on her and ruin her only chance at happiness?

At the thought, Isolde realised that her hands were suddenly trembling. She tightened her grip on her bow, then drew a slow, deep breath until she felt the tension in her body ease and her inner turmoil fade.

If her brother did not give them his blessing, then Orrick would most likely marry her anyway. On that thought she crept back to the bed and, setting her bow and quiver beside her, slipped beneath the pelt and curled against Orrick's side, intending to sleep some more. As the cool morning air acted as a balm to her thoughts, she closed her eyes.

Orrick's arms came around her, warm and sheltering. With him she felt safe, cared for, even . . .

Isolde refused to let the sentiment form. It was too soon for such thoughts. Too many things remained unsettled between them. She knew her purpose. "I defend Scotland as a warrior," she whispered into the silence. She would go to war and fight for what she believed in. Even wounded warriors went on, as she'd discovered at Dunvegan. She had to keep fighting because it was her duty to do so.

But what about Orrick? The man who held her in his arms had left permanent fingerprints on her soul. If he chose not to pick up his sword again, would she be strong enough to fight for both of them when the English came for her?

She knew without a shadow of doubt they would come. And soon. Her time upon this earth might be short. Even so, she would not go out without a fight.

The question was, would Orrick stand with her?

———— ~~~ ————

ALASTAIR AND TORMOD placed torches against two burial pyres that held the remaining bodies of the Englishmen. Night had fallen, and the sky filled with a million stars. Alastair hoped those stars would guide these men to their eternal reward. After reciting an ancient Celtic blessing, Alastair and Tormod returned to the waiting arms of their wives along the shores of Loch Dunvegan as together they watched the flames devour the men's remains. Rowena, Callum, Becks, and Mrs Morgan were there as well. They stood in silence as a light breeze teased the flames to burn hotter and brighter.

They remained on the shore until the flames began to die

down. Alastair pulled Gwendolyn closer, grateful that today had a different ending than the one the dead men had expected.

As though sensing the direction of his thoughts, Gwendolyn turned in his arms. "Do you think Orrick found Izzy?"

"He's the best tracker of us all. I'm certain he did," he said, trying to comfort his wife.

"Then why haven't he and Graeme returned? It's been hours."

"Orrick and Graeme are both wise. They know 'tis safer to travel by daylight."

"We should send out a contingent of men in the morning to make certain no one is watching the castle," Tormod suggested.

Alastair frowned. "I fear our problems once again stem from within our walls not outside of it." He turned to his brother. "Izzy mentioned a white-haired woman in the note she left for Gwendolyn and myself when she left."

Rowena's gaze slid to Alastair's. "I'm not sure how reliable the words of a traumatised child are, but Emlyn claims to have seen that very white-haired woman at the gates moments before they opened."

"Did she say anything more?" Alastair asked, holding back the storm of anger growing inside him. He was so tired of traitors hiding amongst the castle residents.

"You'll have to ask Emlyn. All she said to me was that the woman was tall and pale, with hair as white as snow."

Alastair turned to Gwendolyn. "You know many of the new residents here, especially the females. Does that description match anyone?"

"Nay," Gwendolyn replied, her eyes wide. "Had I seen her, I am sure I would have remembered."

"Rowena, you questioned the reliability of the source of that information, but Izzy saw her as well." Callum's features were partly in shadow from the light of the fading fire.

"Or…" Rowena said, stepping up to the men with a furrowed brow. "Do children and the innocent see things that adults do not?"

Alastair scowled. "Are you suggesting a ghost did this?"

"There is a way to find out. Mother." Callum's voice rang clear in the silence of the night. When nothing happened, he tried again, "Lady Janet!"

This time a swirl of mist appeared along the shoreline, gathering until a luminous woman's body appeared in the darkness. She hovered before them. *There is no need to shout when you need me. Simply call my name and I shall appear, if I am able.*

If she was able? Her choice of words gave Alastair a moment's pause. Their mother had never mentioned such a thing before. He would have to ask her more when things were not so dire. "The young girl, Emlyn, mentioned seeing a tall woman with white hair opening the gates for the English to invade the castle. Do you know of such a person?"

Their mother's already pasty complexion turned white

and fear shone in the Grey Lady's eyes. *The child has seen her?*

"Seen who?" Alastair prompted.

Where is the child? Someone go get Emlyn. There is something you all need to know.

Rowena nodded to Alastair before she hurried towards the sea gate and back to the castle.

"What do we need to know?" Alastair could feel anxiety tightening his shoulders.

"Mother." Tormod moved to stand beside the ghost. "Please explain yourself."

We have a visitor at Dunvegan. A fairy woman who is a descendant of Iain Cair. Or at least she was here until she followed Isolde when she left.

"Our ancestor who was given the Fairy Flag by the fairy princess?" Callum asked incredulously. Alastair could almost see the questions forming behind his younger brother's eyes.

A shiver teased Alastair's neck. The legend of the flag had come to the MacLeods centuries ago. While he believed whole-heartedly in the power the flag possessed, Alastair had always had his doubts that the flag had originated in the fairy realm. "How do you know who she is, Mother?"

She told me so herself when I sensed her presence and confronted her a few days ago. She entered Dunvegan when Orrick brought Isolde back here.

Alastair's heart sped with worry over yet another person creeping past his guards. He would never put anyone else through what his own wife had suffered at the hands of an intruder. As soon as they were done here, he wanted twice as many guards posted at the entrances to the castle and on the towers. "Why didn't you alert us?"

She promised not to harm you. She wanted to get to know her kin better, from a distance, and she had nowhere else to go. She has been alone and wandering since the night of Samhain.

Tormod crossed his arms. "A portal between the human realm and the spirit realm did open on that night. We all felt it, and thought that's when Mother would leave us."

"Instead of Mother leaving, the portal allowed something else to pass through to our world," Callum said.

Alastair's gaze snapped back to his mother's. "Where is she now?"

I do not know. As I said, she left with Isolde.

"So is this a fairy woman, or is she more human than immortal?" Callum pondered with a frown.

Tormod's gaze was severe. "Over the past two weeks since Samhain, the half-fae has proven she can take care of herself."

"By her birthright she is a MacLeod," Fiona said, stepping forward. "Doesn't she deserve the protection of her family? At least until we can learn why she allowed the English inside the gates? There has to be a reason."

Callum's eyes widened. "How old is she? The legend of the flag would put her at over a thousand years old."

Time passes differently in Fairyland than it does here in the human world.

"I say we treat her as a threat until she is proven otherwise," Tormod said, a dark look on his face.

"That is not how we treat guests here at Dunvegan." Gwendolyn's voice rose above the others.

A hush fell amongst them as Rowena returned to the fire with a sleepy Emlyn in tow. "It is how many of us treated Izzy. Me included, which I now regret," Rowena said, her cheeks flushed.

"We are all putting the cart before the horse," Alastair said, his voice firm. "Let us find this woman, then take measure of her. That will tell us how to proceed."

"Where do we find her?" Callum asked. "The isle is large and vast, with many dangers now that not only the clans but also the English are causing unrest."

"If Isolde knows what is best for her, she will have stayed in MacLeod territory." Alastair passed his gaze over those present. He and Tormod could each lead a unit of men. They could use Orrick's help if he returned by daybreak. Even though he was young, Alastair would put Callum in charge of defending the castle. With the support of a large contingent of men, Callum would ensure that everyone inside remained safe.

With a plan in place, Alastair continued, "We can do nothing until first light. I suggest we all go to our beds and take what sleep we can. Tomorrow we will ride in two directions, trying to find not only this woman but also Graeme, Orrick, and Isolde if they do not return before we leave."

CHAPTER FIFTEEN

A S MORNING LIGHT swept inside the cave, forcing the shadows away, Isolde turned to Orrick. He was propped up on his elbow gazing down at her. A smile lit his dark eyes with a rare masculine beauty. Isolde remained silent as she gazed up at the man who would be her husband. A strange sensation curled in her chest. She didn't know what she was feeling at this moment but she knew it was more than contentment.

"Are you well?" Orrick's voice was low as his smile slipped, and a look of concern entered his gaze at her suddenly flushed cheeks.

She drew a shaky breath. "Aye," she whispered. "I don't think I've ever been better. It's just that all this is so new to me, so unexpected."

His concern fled and his eyes twinkled. "It isn't exactly an everyday affair for me either." He bent down and brushed his lips sweetly, tenderly against hers. When he pulled back, he brushed the back of his hand against her jawline. The simple touch communicated support, comfort, serenity. How could one gesture tell her all those things? But somehow it did.

He was gazing at her, his dark eyes softly intent, his expression holding the same breathless wonder she felt.

"Are we certain this marriage will not be a huge mistake for us both?" she asked, breaking the moment.

The warmth of his gaze remained steady. "If I've learned anything over the past few years, it is that one must have faith that all will be well."

"I have faith in you, Orrick, and in the MacLeods. But there are still so many obstacles to overcome. Lieutenant Collins is not a man to take defeat lightly."

"From the shadows in your eyes, I can see your thoughts going in a multitude of directions. Be calm and at peace. You, me, Graeme, and the warriors he brought can meet with your brother and gain his approval while avoiding the English."

"Your family has no idea where you are," Isolde said. "Perhaps we should go our separate ways until we meet up again at Dunvegan."

Orrick shook his head. "Where you go, I go."

After a moment she nodded. "We go together." He enfolded her in his arms and she nestled against him, wanting to stay in this safe, warm moment as long as possible because she couldn't shake the feeling that the world was about to come crashing down around them all.

WHEN DAWN GAVE way to the morning light, Alastair and Tormod were saddled and ready to ride out with a hundred of their men. Callum would remain at Dunvegan with another hundred men to protect those who remained behind.

As Alastair and his men waited for Mrs Honey and her kitchen staff to load the last of the supplies, his attention shifted towards the gate. There, standing before the iron portcullis, was a woman with hair as white as snow and a dress that looked as soft and delicate as the morning mist. Low on her narrow hips, she wore a belt that looked like golden leaves held together with nothing but air.

Alastair dismounted and strode towards the gates despite the bow she held in her hands. She did not raise the weapon to strike as he approached. Up close, he could see the woman's hair was long and straight with small rows of plaits that were gathered around the crown of her head. And her eyes—never had he seen eyes the colour of the sky on a vibrant summer day. She stood still and silent as he stopped before her.

She fit the description Emlyn had given of the woman who had opened the gates to allow the English to enter Dunvegan. "Who are you?" Alastair asked, suddenly noticing that Tormod was beside him.

"My name is Aria." Her voice was whisper-soft, yet filled with strength.

"Why come back here after what you did?" Tormod

asked, his fists as tight as his scowl.

"I came back to warn you of danger."

"Warn us of danger? You should have done as much when you allowed the English inside these walls. We were in danger then. Men suffered and died because of your actions." Alastair felt his pulse throb in his jaw. Why had she come back, and alone? Surely she didn't think she could defend herself with one bow against his one hundred men armed and ready for battle?

Her pale cheeks stained pink. "I am truly sorry for that. I was curious to see what the warrior woman you took in would do against those men. I was watching her. If I hadn't thought she and your men could overcome those thirty soldiers, I never would have done it."

"What if you'd been wrong? What if they'd captured my wife and others?" Alastair asked, his voice hard.

"Then I would have freed them," she said with conviction.

Tormod crossed his arms over his chest as he stared at her. "How can we be certain what you say is true?"

Behind them, a grey mist that had nothing to do with the morning dew rippled across the courtyard until that mist coalesced into the shape of a woman: their mother. *My sons. You should open the gates and allow her to come in. I sense something has changed within her heart and that she belongs with us now.*

"Not until we know more," Tormod said with a frown.

"Do you know this woman, Mother?"

She has been to the castle before. Once recently, and once as a child.

Alastair turned back to the woman separated from him by iron bars. "Before I open this gate, tell me who you are and why you are here."

A flash of pride entered her eyes. "I am Aria MacLeod."

Alastair felt the lines between his brows deepen as he inhaled. His mother had been right about her being kin. "A MacLeod who would harm her own people?" His words ground out with disbelief.

"If you open the gates, I will explain all," Aria said.

For the first time, Alastair saw vulnerability in her wide blue eyes. If she was who she said, it must have taken great courage to return to the gates this morning. "Are you prepared to surrender your weapon?"

She shifted her bow so that it fit through the bars, extending it towards him. "Take it now. I mean you no harm."

"Open the gate." Alastair's voice boomed in the silence that surrounded them. The portcullis opened more slowly than Alastair wanted it to once again, as his impatience flared. The sound of grinding chains and creaking wood filled the morning air. He clenched his fists at his sides as he waited.

When finally the barrier lifted, the woman stepped forward, and handed him her quiver. "My weapons are yours until you see fit to return them."

"Aria MacLeod." Alastair greeted her with a nod as he repeated her name. "And your sire was?" He knew the answer, but wanted to hear it from her lips.

The woman's chin tilted up. "Iain Cair was my father." Her voice was tight, as though it was difficult for her to speak the truth after so long. "After Iain and my mother were married and had a son together, my mother was forced to go back to Fairyland by the fairy king. What she did not know at the time of her return was that she had conceived another child, a daughter. I was born in Fairyland and surrounded by many who loved and cared for me. But something about me was not like the others who lived there. Something was missing inside me." She shook her head. "It is hard to explain."

"Tormod, Orrick, and I understand that feeling. We have lived with it most of our lives," Alastair said, sympathising with her suffering. "Our father was not a kind or gentle man. We all left Dunvegan for years, trying to find ourselves." Alastair released a soft chuckle at the sudden realisation his words brought. "Yet we all had to return to Dunvegan to find ourselves. And, now here you are, hoping for the same."

"That is a lovely story," Tormod interrupted. "You expect us to believe that you are part MacLeod, and part fairy? And that you came here to find yourself, but instead of helping your kin, you nearly destroyed them?"

Aria's features darkened. "The fairy part of me is strong.

That's all I've known for years. It is full of mischief and mayhem. Over time, and with much discipline, I will be able to keep it in check. I am so sorry for what I did, and when I witnessed what happened after I let the English past your gates, I tried to help. Five of the men who died that day did so because of my arrows."

Alastair considered the truth of her words. There had been unusual arrows deep in the chests of some of the men they had sent on to their reward. "Why come to us today speaking of danger?"

There is danger. I sensed it as well. The English are not through with the MacLeods just yet, I fear. Their mother floated in a tight circle as if her pent-up energy demanded she move.

Tormod shook his head. "I heard that Izzy forced a promise out of the lieutenant to leave the MacLeods in peace."

"Lieutenant Collins is not to be trusted. He will do only what is best for him and his advancement in the military hierarchy to which he belongs." Aria's gaze slid between the two brothers. "I saw him heading towards Scorrybreac Castle. The look in his eyes was that of revenge."

"Did Izzy go back there? Is Orrick with her?" Alastair asked, his gaze penetrating.

"Nay. There were only Englishmen."

"Then Orrick must still be searching for Izzy," Tormod said.

"Or following Izzy back to Scorrybreac," Alastair suggested.

Tormod turned to Aria. "You didn't follow?"

She shook her head. "Instead, I came to tell you what I saw so you could decide how to proceed. The woman you call Izzy might be in danger. She might not. When I saw you and your men preparing to leave, I wanted you to know where the English were."

"How many men did Lieutenant Collins have?" Alastair asked, trying to formulate a plan of action before they set out.

"Somewhere between forty and fifty," Aria said. "Lieutenant Collins's company suffered significant losses after their attack on this castle."

"Then that is one good thing that came from the attack," Alastair said as his brow furrowed in thought. "You'll need to explain where they are so that we can find them, then you can remain here while we are gone."

"Nay," Aria objected. "I want to go with you, to help you, because only then will I find a different life for myself."

Alastair knew what it was like to want something different. "What is it that you want?"

Her mouth quirked. "Something I never thought I'd have. To find my purpose here in the human realm. I was shunned by the other fairies for being half-human. They said I was clumsy, heavy-footed, and without talent."

Alastair's gaze passed over her once more. The woman

appeared as soft and ethereal as the mist. He released a slow, even breath, considering his options. Then raised her bow. "Are you any good with a weapon?"

"That, none of the fairies ever complained about. I am a superb archer," Aria said with a smile.

"And modest," Tormod grumbled.

She shrugged. "I can demonstrate my skill if you'd like."

Alastair handed Aria back her bow and quiver. Something deep in his gut told him he could trust her.

"Choose a target," she said while looping the string at the end of her bow.

Alastair looked about him. "How about the tree over there?" He pointed back towards the gardens.

"Too easy." She frowned. "Does anyone have an apple?" she asked the gathered men behind Alastair and Tormod.

An 'aye' came from the back of those on horseback.

"Throw it into the air as high as you can." Her voice was clear and filled with confidence.

The apple went up, towering over the heads of the men. Before it could come back towards the ground, Aria effortlessly plucked an arrow from her quiver and speared the apple in mid-air. The apple and arrow fell to the ground with a thump.

"Impressive," Alastair said. She'd not only hit a moving target, but a small target at that.

"You're quite good," Tormod acknowledged begrudgingly.

"We'll need another horse saddled for Aria," Alastair called to one of the stable boys who remained nearby. He nodded and hurried back to the stable. A few minutes later he emerged leading a white mare.

Alastair had to admit, it seemed the perfect choice. Aria atop a white horse would only add to her ethereal image. Alastair offered her his hand to help her up into the saddle, before he and Tormod mounted and came up beside her. "Welcome to the family, Aria MacLeod. I apologise that your first adventure with your clan is to find our missing brother and possibly go to war with the English."

"Conquering everyone and everything. Isn't that what MacLeods were raised to do?" Aria asked as her horse fell into step between Alastair and Tormod as they started through the gates.

Alastair chuckled. "Perhaps in the past. My brothers and I are trying to walk a different path."

"And what path is that?" she asked.

"We tried diplomacy and cooperation but unfortunately, we appear to be circling back to war," Alastair said with a frown.

"Do you still possess the Fairy Flag that my mother left your clan?" Aria asked.

"We do," Alastair said. "Though we can only use it one more time before the flag will return to the fairy world along with the person holding it."

"Do you carry it with you today?" She looked at the contingent of men at her back.

"Nay," Alastair replied. "Only when it seems as if there is no hope for all of Scotland will I use the magic the flag possesses."

"Then it's a fair thing you are riding into a possible battle alongside a fairy," she said with a smile.

"Half a fairy," Tormod corrected.

Aria rolled her eyes. "Half a fairy is better than no fairy at all."

CHAPTER SIXTEEN

I SOLDE AND ORRICK arrived at the gates of Scorrybreac Castle later that afternoon. They were taking a risk of harming the MacLeod clan's relationship with the Nicolson clan, but it was something Isolde felt strongly about. She might have been banished for not acting as her brother would prefer she did and not accepting his choice of a husband for her, but John was the only family she had left in this world. His approval of her marriage meant everything to her.

That didn't mean the moments ahead of them would be easy. John was still a possible threat. So far, their journey to Scorrybreac had been blessedly free of incident. They'd seen no sign of English troops along the way. Was it too much to hope that Lieutenant Collins and his remaining men had headed back to England?

While they'd travelled on horseback together, Isolde was keenly aware through the movements of his body that Orrick observed every cluster of trees, shrubbery, and rock outcropping. It wasn't until they came to the gates before them that his shoulders relaxed ever so slightly. He was still tense when

Isolde announced who they were and asked for admittance into the castle to see her brother.

"You look almost relieved," Orrick said from behind her, on the horse they shared, as the gates opened, allowing Orrick, Isolde, Graeme, and the other MacLeod warriors entrance.

"Until this moment, I wasn't sure John would actually see me," Isolde replied as they entered the bailey and were met by a dozen soldiers. She instantly recognised Watt, Murdo, and Richard, her previous tormentors, at the front of the group. Isolde met their startled and angry gazes with a steely look of her own. She wasn't the same person who had left here over a year ago. They no longer held any sort of power over her. For she had proven to herself that she could thrive on her own.

Orrick must have noticed the men's gazes himself because his jaw firmed, his back straightened, and he became even more formidable under her gaze. Orrick dismounted and then helped her down before handing over his horse to a waiting stable boy. Graeme and his men did the same.

"Come," Watt said as the men surrounded them on their approach to the keep. "I'm sure you remember the way."

It felt strange to be back home after so long away. It was as if she were seeing the castle through new eyes. The walls of the outer bailey had always looked old, but now they were pitted and in desperate need of repair. Isolde frowned at the thought that her brother had not tended the ancient structure as he should have over the past year. They headed for the courtyard. There, servants carried pitchforks of hay towards the stables where the cattle awaited their meal. Instead of relaxed and carefree as she remembered them, the very same servants appeared tired, stooped, and looked at the ground instead of at her.

The clang of the smithy pounding steel punctuated the air in an irregular beat, causing several of the women carrying yeasty bread from the brick oven to the kitchen shed to startle when the hammer hit metal. As she and Orrick strode past, she could feel their gazes upon her.

Isolde ignored them. John knew her well enough to know she would return someday despite his banishment if she discovered Sarah's child had lived. Though the others probably never expected to see her again. When she, Orrick, and the others entered the keep and made their way to the great hall, Isolde's own nervousness took hold. How would her brother greet her? Would Sarah and the child be there? Until that moment, she hadn't realised how much she wanted to meet her niece. If only they would grant her that wish.

Inside the chamber, the men surrounding them shifted back against the walls, allowing Isolde, Orrick, Graeme and the men to move freely towards the laird who stood, waiting at the top of the dais. A hush fell over the chamber.

"You look different than I remember you," her brother said in the way of a greeting. No smile. No warmth. Just a statement.

Isolde stood proud with her bow in her hand and her quiver at her back. "I accept myself for who I am now. That is the only change I know of."

Her brother, John, looked older than she remembered. Grey now threaded his brown hair and concentrated at his temples. Isolde shuddered as a chill moved through her. Were the events of that fateful day responsible for this change in him? Needing to say the words that had festered inside her for so long, she stopped before her brother and met his gaze. "I am so sorry your family was injured by my arrow, John. I have prayed for your safety and welfare every day since I left."

From behind her brother, Sarah stepped out into the open with a child in her arms. "Your prayers were not heard," her brother's wife said angrily. There was no forgiveness in her eyes, only pain. "We suffer now more than ever because of you."

"Sarah." John's voice was hard.

Sarah stiffened, but remained beside her husband. In Sarah's arms, Brea squirmed, wanting to be set down. As she squiggled, the hem of her gown came up, exposing one perfectly formed leg and another that was red and purple and swollen. The scent of rotting flesh came to Isolde as she narrowed her gaze on the little girl's leg. The appendage was not deformed as Isolde had expected. The leg was putrid and rotting. Her gaze shifted to Sarah's. Did they not realise that was what was happening? Why didn't they do something to help their little girl?

"Why come back here?" John asked, bringing Isolde's gaze back to him. His face was tense and the wariness in his eyes made her ache. "What do you want? And why bring Orrick MacLeod and his men with you?"

Instead of answering his questions, she asked her own. "Why is the castle in such a state of disrepair, and why haven't you sought a healer or a barber for your daughter? Surely you see what is happening to her."

John looked disconcerted, then angry. "Of course I see how she suffers. But we have been choked off from the outside world for the past year by the English, thanks to you. We are their prisoners."

"The English are here? Inside the gates?" Orrick asked, his hand moving to the hilt of his sword. Graeme and the others did the same.

John paled as his gaze flew to Orrick's then Graeme's. "The English are outside the gates, but they make their presence known if we try to leave. They have allowed small hunting parties to exit the castle occasionally, but that is all."

Sensing the threat was not imminent, Orrick and the others relaxed their hold on their weapons.

"I had no idea." Isolde's breath caught as she imagined the horror these people must have endured for the months since she'd escaped Lieutenant Collins and his men. They had been isolated every bit as much as she had. "Did you ever try to send word to other clans while your men were outside the castle?"

John shook his head. "We were watched very closely."

She gaped at her brother. "You never challenged these English soldiers?"

"Nay," John replied. "There were too many of them."

Isolde was suddenly furious that her brother had never even tried to break free of someone holding him and his people captive. "Never do you give the enemy that much power over you. Even faced with inconceivable odds, you fight back. That is what Father and Alaric taught us." Isolde looked about the chamber. "Where is Alaric? Surely he would have led you into battle."

"Alaric left us shortly after you did. He was angry with me for sending you away. He took it upon himself to search for you, wherever you had gone." Her brother's gaze dropped to the ground. "Since you ask that question, I assume he never found you."

"Nay. He never did." As she looked about the chamber, Isolde's gaze lit on a curious sight. An arrow hung on the wall just above the doorway that led in and out of the great hall. "What is that?" She angled her head towards the arrow.

"That is the arrow you shot Sarah with, the arrow that put her into labour, the arrow that harmed my child." He stared at Isolde angrily. "I put it there so that all of us might remember who we had to blame for our current circumstances."

Isolde put her hands on her hips. "You cannot blame me for your lack of action, Brother. Only yourself. If I were here, I would have fought the English, all alone if no one else had joined me. I would rather have gone to my death knowing I tried to make my life better than letting despair choke me."

She turned and strode through the hall back to the door. There she stood on her toes and stretched to take the arrow down before bringing it back to her brother. "This arrow is not responsible for your—" She looked down at the arrowhead and her heart stumbled. "The steel . . . there is a tiny piece missing." She shoved the arrow into her brother's hands and moved to Sarah and her niece.

Orrick joined her, watching her intently. "What are you thinking, Isolde?"

"The injury to her leg. I may know what is wrong. Might I have a look at Brea's leg?" Isolde asked Sarah.

Sarah startled. "You know her name?"

"Rowena MacLeod told me. Might I take a look at her wound? I might be able to help her."

The anger and pain in Sarah's features were replaced with hope. She held Brea out to Isolde.

Isolde carried the child to the long table behind them all, and set her down, stretching her out to study her leg.

"What can I do?" Orrick asked, stepping away from Graeme and the others.

"Distract her while I check her leg."

"That, I can do." Orrick smiled down at the curious little girl. "Hello, my sweet. Now you see me." Then he covered his face. "Now you don't." A moment later, he uncovered his face and looked at Brea with wide eyes and an open-mouthed smile. "Surprise." The little girl gave a full-bellied chuckle in response.

As the two of them continued the game, Isolde examined the child's leg, then shifted her gaze between John and Sarah. "I believe a part of that arrowhead is still inside Brea's leg. It's presumably been there since her birth." Isolde drew a breath. "I know you have no reason to trust me, but I am begging you to do so at this moment. While in the wilderness, I studied nature and learned many things." She reached down and pulled her *sgian-dubh* from her boot. "Someone warm this blade in the fire until it glows red."

"I'll do it," Sarah said, taking the knife. "I don't trust you, but I want my child to live." She turned to John and said, "If we don't do something soon, we'll have to cut off her leg in order to save her."

John nodded.

"I'll also need some linen for a bandage, a cloth to place under her leg to absorb the blood, and some whisky."

John sent someone to find what she needed. While Sarah was away, Isolde found a water basin and washed her hands.

When the linen arrived, Isolde slid it under the child, keeping a long length for a bandage. Sarah returned the small dagger to Isolde. She allowed the blade to cool. Then, with a warning glance at Orrick who stopped his game and instead held the little girl's arm and legs still, Isolde scraped away the rotting flesh until she found an area where the pus and drainage seemed to originate. Isolde placed her arm across the little girl's injured leg and leaned down, pinning her to the table so she could not move. Brea started to cry even as Orrick tried his best to distract her. Knowing it had to be done, Isolde steeled herself, then inserted the blade into the putrid area little by little until blood flowed freely instead of only pus.

Brea cried out, now more stridently. Sarah came to comfort her, and John came over and held the child's leg so Isolde could manoeuvre better.

Deep inside the child's leg muscles, Isolde finally saw something that didn't belong. Something shiny and hard. The metal fragment. She removed it, then inspected it to make certain it was the missing piece and that no other fragments remained behind. Satisfied that she had retrieved the only arrow fragment, Isolde breathed a sigh of relief, before reaching for the whisky and pouring it over the wound, cleansing it.

Brea cried all the harder for a long moment as the whisky entered her wound, but then after a short while her sobs lessened, then quieted.

Isolde took advantage of the momentary stillness to wrap the long length of linen around Brea's little leg. "Normally, I would stich the wound, but leaving it open will help it fully drain. When the wound starts to heal, spread honey over it daily," Isolde told Sarah.

Sarah scooped her daughter into her arms and held her tightly. "Where did you learn all this?"

"In the wilderness, as I said, and also from the Mac-Leods' healer, Lottie." Isolde pushed aside her cloak and exposed her injured arm to her brother and sister-in-law. "There is a long story behind this, but needless to say, I understand what Brea was going through just now."

"If we gather your men and mount an attack against the English, then you'd be free to travel back to Dunvegan with us. Lottie would be pleased to watch over your daughter until she returns to full health," Orrick offered.

"Attack the English? We haven't been able to do so for a year." The earlier shadows returned to John's features. "Why did you come here? I'm certain it wasn't because of Brea's leg, for you didn't know about that until you arrived."

Orrick reached out and enfolded Isolde's hand in his larger one. He moved closer. For a moment she felt as if they were joined in an intimacy more complete than the one they had shared in the night. The Nicolson part of her merged with the MacLeod part of him and the two of them were reborn as one, even without her brother's blessing or that of a minister. "I come to ask for your sister's hand in marriage."

With an effort, Isolde pulled her gaze away from the man at her side and watched as a barrage of emotions flickered across her brother's face—surprise, shock, anxiety, then fear.

Why would he fear her marrying a MacLeod?

Or was he afraid of her marrying anyone other than that fool Ewen MacPhee? Her connection to Ewen had been severed as far as she was concerned by the man's deliberate cheating. She owed him nothing.

"I must say, I am surprised that anyone would have you, Isolde." He shrugged. "If that is what the MacLeod wants, and if you are willing, then what can I say beside 'aye'? You have my blessing."

Instead of relief, she felt a sharp pain. She lowered her lashes to hide her eyes. Her brother still knew how to hurt her with his carefully chosen words. *I'm surprised anyone would have you.* He might have given his approval, but it was not given out of love. And suddenly, she wanted to be gone from Scorrybreac. Even the wilderness was preferable to her brother's home. "Thank you, John," she forced out. "We will be leaving now."

"Nay." The word erupted violently from him. "Nay," he said more softly. "First we must go to the chapel and tell Mother and Father the news."

She frowned at her brother. They'd had a memorial marker made and placed in the chapel after their parents had died, their bodies lost at sea. The marble memorial was that of a winged angel sitting on a stone chest that had been engraved with their parents' names. Both she and John had gone to the chapel and sat on the chest beside the angel and talked to their parents, telling them everything. It made sense that he would want her to do so now, yet she didn't miss the slight tremor that shook her brother before he set his chin a little higher.

Isolde frowned. Or was she imagining things that weren't there? With a sigh, Isolde nodded. At least she could introduce Orrick to her parents in the only possible way at the memorial.

"Come with me, Orrick and Isolde, but your men should remain here. We won't be gone long."

Graeme frowned. "We should come with you."

"All is well, Graeme. This will only take a moment. Besides, no harm can come to us in a chapel."

Reluctantly, Graeme nodded, but continued to frown as John escorted them out of the great hall and down a long hallway that led to another door that would take them outside. The chapel was not connected to the main keep, as it had been added after the main structure had been built. Torches lit the way as the same twelve guards accompanied John and the two of them down the hallway.

While they walked, Orrick leaned close and whispered, "If the English have been watching Scorrybreac, then we must assume we've been observed arriving at this castle."

"Agreed," Isolde whispered back. "Be on guard." In the next moment, John stopped unexpectedly and spun around with a sword in his hands.

"It's a trap!" Isolde cried, but her warning came too late.

Before Orrick could reach for his sword, Watt surged

forward, jamming the hilt of his sword into Orrick's solar plexus with such force that it robbed him of air as he stumbled back, separating him from Isolde.

She lunged forward, but not before a gate dropped from the ceiling in front of and another behind Orrick and slammed against the floor. Time seemed to still as Isolde's heart thundered in her ears. She had trusted her brother and look where that had gotten her. She should have known something wasn't right. There had been one clue after another since they'd entered the castle, but she hadn't wanted to believe what was before her eyes. Her hand moved to the hilt of her sword.

Graeme and the others must have heard her cries because footsteps sounded behind Orrick. Perhaps they could help free the two of them.

Behind her, the door to the outside slammed open, crashing with violence against the wall on the other side. In the narrow hallway, the English soldiers rushed in. Isolde only got in one swipe before they were on her, knocking the sword from her hands. Lieutenant Collins forced his way forward, dragging his damaged leg. He grabbed Isolde's injured arm and hurled her to the ground with such bruising force that her bow flew from her hand and out of her reach.

"This time you'll not get the chance to make a fool out of me." He grinned at her wolfishly, ready to exact his revenge.

CHAPTER SEVENTEEN

ORRICK'S BREATH WAS still caught in his throat and pain radiated across his chest, but if he didn't get out of this trap now, he, Graeme, the men, and Isolde would all be killed by the English and the Nicolsons. Orrick kicked out ferociously against the metal bars, feeling them give just a little.

"What are you doing? Stop that," a man with a bushy beard said, drawing his sword and poking it through the bars.

Orrick jumped out of range as he looked up at the ceiling. The gates had been hastily installed, which was to his benefit. As the man withdrew his sword to thrust it once more, Orrick drew back and kicked again. Four times they played the game of thrust and retreat before the iron grate fell away, releasing Orrick. Graeme and his men battled their way through those who had imprisoned Orrick, but he didn't wait for them. He had to catch up to Isolde.

In that moment, all of Orrick's reserves about fighting evaporated. The person he was before leaving for the West Indies pulsed through his blood, heightening his awareness to the threats around him as he surged forward. He scooped up Isolde's bow, then raced out the door, hoping he wasn't too late to catch sight of her. The English wouldn't punish her here at Scorrybreac where she still might have sympathisers. Nay, they would take her somewhere they controlled the situation.

He and Graeme and the men had to hurry to escape the castle as well. Even as MacLeods, the Nicolson men might turn on them as they had Isolde. Orrick ran through the courtyard and into the bailey where his thoughts were confirmed. The Englishmen retreated through the open gates with a blond-haired female. Isolde was gagged and her hands were tied before her as she rode on a horse in front of Lieutenant Collins.

Orrick sent out a shrill whistle. Even in a stall, Phoenix would escape when Orrick used that particular whistle. And just as he expected, a few moments later, Phoenix emerged from the stables, except that instead of charging, he was led out by John Nicolson and several of his men who also brought the other MacLeod horses.

Orrick's hand moved to the hilt of his sword. If he had to, he would fight his way out of this castle. His brow furrowed when he noticed none of the Nicolsons had their weapons drawn. As they came closer, Orrick could see deep lines around John's eyes and mouth. The look was not nervousness. It was worry.

Orrick stood with his feet apart and his hand on the hilt

of his sword, but he did not draw his weapon. If John wanted to talk, he would hear him out. Quickly. "If you are here as a friend, release my horse. If foe, then prepare to die."

"What they say about the MacLeods is true, and I can see why my sister finds you a mutual spirit. You are warriors like no others. You'd truly take on my one hundred men with only a small contingent?" John Nicolson smiled.

Orrick scowled. "If I had to in order to save Isolde from certain death."

"Peace. We are not here to fight you." John released Phoenix's reins and the horse came to Orrick. "I had no idea the Englishmen would capture her. Lieutenant Collins simply said he wished to talk with her."

Orrick swung up into his saddle. He turned to John. "You were foolish enough to believe that?"

John flinched, then pressed his lips into a hard line. "Lieutenant Collins and his men have been terrorising us for months. What I said about being a prisoner within these walls was true. He threatened to choke off our food supply and everything else if I didn't cooperate with him and his men." John paused as sadness filled his gaze. "He said nothing about capturing my sister. I had no idea he'd built that trap. He demanded I get Isolde to go to the chapel when an English patrol saw you both approaching Scorrybreac. We had time to prepare for your arrival. I thought Lieutenant Collins only meant to talk with Isolde there."

Orrick's gaze raked the man before him. "Trusting others

is an admirable trait, except when it comes to the enemy."

"Am I your enemy?" John asked, his tone harsh.

"Not if you and your men come with me and my men to rescue your sister." Impatience flared in Orrick's chest. They had to go, and quickly, if they were to see what direction the English had taken Isolde. Danger was gathering in the very air, and Orrick didn't necessarily want to stop it this time.

At John's nod of approval, the MacLeod men who had caught up to Orrick and the Nicolsons mounted their horses and rode through the gates of Scorrybreac. Orrick allowed himself a moment to remember Isolde when she'd awoken that morning. He recalled how lovely she'd looked with tousled hair and fewer shadows in her blue eyes. Lying there beside her, he'd never been happier in his life. When he'd first returned to Dunvegan he'd felt dead inside, numb to all that was around him. His only pleasure had come from his books.

Isolde had changed all that. She challenged him to once again be the warrior he was born to be. He was a MacLeod, after all. Their father had claimed his sons, his triplets, would one day be the strength Scotland needed to remain united in her purpose—to fight for what was right and true and just.

Orrick wanted nothing more than to fight for Scotland with Isolde at his side. He kicked his horse into a faster gait when he caught a blur of the enemy's red coats in the distance, heading east.

No longer did Orrick doubt that he was a warrior, and

equal to the task of defeating the English who had taken Isolde prisoner. He would never abandon anyone who needed his help, especially not the woman he loved. His throat tightened at the thought. He did love her, with all his heart, and that was something worth fighting and dying for.

GREY CLOUDS BILLOWED overhead, bathing the world around Isolde in a strange half-light. "Where are we going?" she asked the man behind her, keeping her body stiff so as not to lean against Lieutenant Collins's chest.

He laughed. "A special place where I can do anything I like to you for killing so many of my men. It seems only fair that we should exact our revenge upon you."

A cold, clawing fear moved though her at the satisfaction in his voice. Lieutenant Collins wouldn't kill her quickly. Somehow she knew he would take his time with her, maximising her pain until she begged for release. And he would push her even beyond that point. But his delay in killing her might also be her salvation. The cage they'd trapped Orrick in was not going to stop him from coming after her. The only question was, would he be able to raise his sword against their enemy when he did?

Lieutenant Collins and his men rode in silence for a distance before they turned to the north. As they did, Isolde listened for hoofbeats following them. When the sound couldn't be heard, her throat tightened and her vision clouded. She tilted her chin up and kept her back straight, refusing to give in to her tears. Orrick would come for her. He had to because she wasn't certain she would be able to fight her way out of this situation. She'd lost her bow and her sword. Unless she could somehow untie her hands and relieve one of these men of their weapon, she was unarmed. But not defenceless. She would fight until there was no fight left inside her.

They'd been riding for at least an hour when the remains of a long-abandoned castle appeared in the distance. As they approached, she could see that the English company had set up camp near the old structure. "Welcome to *Caisteal an Bhàis*," the lieutenant drawled. The Castle of Death.

He stopped his horse before the structure, then dismounted. With a tug on her leg, he pulled her off the horse. With no hands to break her fall, Isolde hit her head on the ground. She shook off the dizziness that followed as two men came forward and yanked her to her feet. She worked at the rope binding her hands, twisting them back and forth in an effort to free herself.

The men in red jackets escorted her to a narrow staircase, leading up to a tower that, despite the ruined state of the rest of the castle, appeared to be intact. The light inside the tower was dim and she struggled to see through the gloom. Once Isolde's eyes adjusted to the low light, she could see doorways off to her right as they passed by, heading to the third floor.

There, one man opened a door while the other thrust her inside.

The blaze of light in the chamber temporarily blinded Isolde. She stood blinking for several long moments until she could finally see a dozen or more candles had been lit in sconces around the walls. Silhouetted against the glare, Isolde saw two figures—one tall and well-built, the other short and stooped. The tall man wore a red military jacket. Most likely someone from the lieutenant's company. The other man wore a plain brown robe. When he turned towards her, his mouth twisted into a slow smile of satisfaction.

It was then that her eyes drifted towards a long table and beside it a smaller one lined with metal tools. Isolde swallowed hard, feeling as though flint had been jammed in her throat, stopping her breath. The lieutenant meant to make his retribution as slow and as painful as possible—not with battle, but with torture.

With renewed intensity, she worked her hands, trying to break free. Once they tied her to that table, she would be utterly at their mercy.

"I have no secrets to tell you. So why torture me?" Isolde asked, stalling as she felt the ropes begin to loosen.

The stooped man's smile grew. "I care not about what secrets you harbour. I am merely here to make certain you confess to being an enemy to the crown. With your confession, the lieutenant will have every right to execute you without trial."

Isolde forced her features to go as hard as steel. Showing any kind of fear would give these men an advantage over her. The ropes at her wrists cut through her flesh, leaving a stinging, biting pain that was nothing compared to what awaited her on that table.

The stooped man moved to his tools and motioned to the man in the chamber and the others at the door. "Get her on the table." The three of them came towards her just as she pulled free of her bonds. She snapped one man in the face with the cord that had bound her, surprising him and sending him jerking backwards. Of the two remaining men, one grabbed her shoulders while the other charged. Using the man behind her for stability, she grasped his arms, then lifting her legs, kicked the other man in the gut with all her force. She sent him stumbling backwards with a howl of pain. He bumped into the man she'd whipped in the face and sent him sprawling down the stairs.

Instead of fighting the man at her back, she brought her feet down and pushed him backwards, into the wall of the chamber. His startled breath exploded next to her ear. She didn't give him a chance to draw another breath before she stomped her heel down on the instep of his foot and brought her elbow up to bash him in the nose. He released his grip on her.

She ran for the door, but not before the man she'd kicked recovered. He drew his sword and charged. Isolde twisted out of the way, sending the man's blade into the chest of the man who had released her. Taking advantage of his momentary shock, she kicked the man with the sword in the jaw, feeling bone shatter. He gave a choked cry.

Isolde ripped the sword from his hands and bashed him in the side of the head with the hilt. He collapsed on top of the other soldier he had killed.

The only man left standing stared at her, his long face pale and his eyes filled with fear. Instead of fighting her, he held out his hands, pressed together at the wrists, for her to tie. "Don't hurt me. I'll stay quiet. You can leave here and no one will be the wiser."

He might be a torturer, but he was certainly also a coward. Isolde removed the soldiers' cross belts and tied the stooped man's hands, then gagged him with a strip of fabric torn from the man's own cloak. Then, just to make certain he stayed silent, she hit him in the head with the hilt of her confiscated sword. She tied the other men up as well, and with an effort pulled the man who had fallen down the stairs back up into the tower chamber before shutting the door. None of them would be missed for a while.

It gave her time to figure out what to do next. She would never be able to fight her way through the whole English company. Not by herself. So instead of going down the stairs, she climbed to the top of the tower. On the roof, she stayed low so as not to be seen, and peered over the side. All around the tower, Lieutenant Collins's men had set up their tents, leaving no open space for her to make her escape.

Below, she counted seven and fifty men milling about, and those were the ones she could see. There would be more in the tents or off on patrols who could return at any time. Isolde pressed her lips into a thin, flat line. She could wait until dark to try to make her escape. Except that someone might come up to the tower to relieve the other guards, or Lieutenant Collins might come himself to check on the progress of her torture. She wouldn't put it past him to do so. He enjoyed watching others suffer.

Nay, she couldn't take the chance of waiting. Even if she silently eliminated anyone who entered the tower, one by one. Eventually they would grow suspicious that no one came out, and again she would be more than outnumbered when they attacked.

Her best option was to take her chances sneaking out, finding a way past the men and the tents, until she could disappear once more into the wilderness. Had she known what the day might bring, she would have stayed in bed beside Orrick a little longer this morning. She would have embraced him one last time, savouring the feel of his chest pressed close to her own. She would have given him one last kiss, not a kiss filled with fire, only tenderness so that he might know how very dear to her he had become.

He had asked her to marry him. And for the rest of that night and into the morning, the thought that they would actually join their lives had filled her with both trepidation and joy. But now she knew there would be no marriage. No further merging of their bodies. No future for her other than that of a woman alone, but not quite as lonely as before. For she would keep her memories of Orrick close to her heart.

At a sound in the distance, Isolde's heart stilled. Hoofbeats. A sea of green and blue mixed with a familiar red and green. A surge of hope so powerful moved through her that it stole her breath.

Could it be Orrick and his men along with her brother and his men? Or was desperation making her see and hear things that weren't there? She dropped her gaze to the Englishmen below. If it was only her imagination, then why were the Englishmen racing to gather their weapons?

Isolde lifted her gaze to the distance and saw more clearly the man she'd feared she would never see again. *Orrick.*

She tightened her hand on her sword and charged back into the tower and down the stairs. She would do whatever it took to fight her way back into his life.

CHAPTER EIGHTEEN

*I*SOLDE. ORRICK HAD to get to her before something terrible happened. He kicked his horse into a faster gait as he caught sight of her blond hair. She battled four soldiers on her own with only a sword, and others were gathering their weapons preparing to confront not only John, Graeme, and their small army, but also Isolde. Somehow she had managed to get herself free of her bonds. Orrick allowed himself a momentary smile. And regardless of the odds, she would fight for her freedom.

At the end of the English encampment, Orrick turned to John and Graeme. "*Alba gu brath*," he said. Scotland forever. "Take the men and subdue the English with their warriors. I'll get to Isolde and keep her safe." On Phoenix's back, Orrick shot forward, through the tents. Nothing would keep him from finding Isolde.

"Isolde," he called out, wanting her to know he was there, that she was not alone in this battle. The moment he entered the encampment, he'd lost sight of her so he listened instead for the sound of battle in the distance where he had seen her last. Men challenged him as he progressed. The round targe on his forearm warded off the men's strikes at him and his horse. From atop Phoenix, Orrick had the advantage. He could easily strike the English soldiers down or kick them with his boots, sending them tumbling into each other. By the time they regained their footing, he'd passed by.

All around him the screech and clangour of steel, the grunts of mutual exertion, the noisy inhalations and exhalations of the men battling sounded. Time slowed, allowing Orrick to see each move before it was made, to decipher the manoeuvres of his opponent, to position himself to better advantage. He'd learned all that in the West Indies. The last part of him that had died in that foreign land was reborn. He had only truly begun to live as he wanted and he would not die anytime soon, God willing.

He was a MacLeod. He was born to be a warrior. He believed in courting peace whenever possible, but he could and would take a life if there was no other way forward. And he would do whatever it took to find Isolde and keep her safe.

———— ∿ ————

THE SWORD FELL from Isolde's hand as a heavy blow bashed against her head. She had no time to call out to Orrick. She'd heard him calling her name. She had no time to run. Instead, she fell to the ground beside her sword. She tried to reach out for the weapon, but it was hastily kicked out of her reach.

"I'll not give you a chance to attack me again," Lieutenant Collins's voice cut through the dizziness crowding her thoughts. He bent down beside her, intending to tie her hands.

Isolde kicked and writhed, desperate to get away, to find her way to freedom even as the lieutenant's hands grasped her own, binding them with a heavy cord.

"Quit fighting me and this will go a lot easier for you," the lieutenant said with a scowl.

"Never." She dug her fingernails into the vice-grip that held her until she drew blood. The man grunted, then brought his hand down against her cheek with angry force. The impact sent her senses reeling. Black edged her vision. She drew several short, sharp breaths through her nose, trying desperately to stay conscious. When she could gather her breath in her lungs, she cried out, "Orrick!"

"Damn you, little wench!" Lieutenant Collins yelled.

He hit her again. But this time, Isolde drew on reserves of strength to stay conscious. She'd not make it easy for the lieutenant to exact his revenge. She had to give Orrick time to find her.

In the next moment, Lieutenant Collins's lips pulled up in a grin as he forced a foul-smelling piece of linen into her mouth. He tied the cloth securely behind her head. The need to gag overwhelmed her, but she pushed it aside and lashed out against her attacker. He might have tied her hands and silenced her, but he had not won the battle.

Lieutenant Collins yanked on her arm and hauled her to her feet, then he propelled her towards a waiting horse. He tossed her onto the horse's back before mounting behind her. Kicking the animal into a run, he headed away from the encampment and towards the cliffs near the coastline.

At their rapid pace, Isolde could do nothing but grasp at the horse's mane with her fingers and hold on. Her captor seemed unimpressed by the steep cliff off to their right and the loose path beneath the horse's feet as he encouraged his mount to greater speed.

Fear roiled in Isolde's stomach, but she lifted her chin as they skirted the cliff's edge. Ahead of them, a craggy rock formation rose, forcing the lieutenant to veer inland to go around it. The crumbling rock beneath the horse's hooves forced the animal to slow its pace, and with it, afforded Isolde a little more time to come up with a plan of escape.

As though reading her thoughts, the lieutenant gripped her more tightly around the waist, pulling her hard against his front. "There will be no escape for you. I've waited a year to exact my revenge on you and I will not be denied a second time."

A shiver of fear moved through Isolde. Once the lieutenant stopped his horse, she would most likely face her death.

ORRICK DIDN'T STOP to think about what he was doing. After dismounting, he reached for his sword and ran straight into the heart of the battle, desperate to reach Isolde. He headed towards the tower where he'd seen her last.

He didn't break his hurried stride as he cut down one soldier after another, desperate to reach her. At the tower he battled two men before he came upon a third dressed in a brown robe, like that of a monk. The man was unarmed. Instead of slicing him down, Orrick sheathed his sword and gripped the man by the throat, pressing him back against the tower wall. "Where is Isolde?"

The man stared at Orrick, his mouth slack.

"Where did the lieutenant take Isolde?" Orrick repeated more harshly.

The man motioned to the right with his eyes.

Orrick released the man's throat. "More details."

After sucking in a breath, the man frowned and rubbed his throat that now bore the red imprint of Orrick's hand. "You'll never catch Lieutenant Collins in time. He took the girl to the cliffs to execute her."

Orrick sent out a shrill whistle, calling Phoenix to his side. "Where is the lieutenant's tent? Show me. Quickly."

"This way." The man darted ahead of Orrick and led him past several tents until they reached a larger, grander one. "What are you looking for?"

Orrick forced the man inside the tent's opening. "The quiver the lieutenant took from his captive."

"Over there," the man said, pointing to where the container of arrows lay atop a small desk.

Orrick scooped up the quiver and put it over his shoulder before grasping the bow, then turned for the door.

"You'll never catch them in time," the man in brown robes called as Orrick pushed the tent flap open.

Without a hitch in his step, Orrick kept going. The man obviously didn't know the will of a MacLeod when someone they loved was in trouble. Outside the tent, Phoenix waited. Orrick was up in the saddle and heading towards the cliffs, forcing the pain that constricted his chest away. He would not allow himself to have doubts. Isolde needed him.

Behind him, a second set of hoofbeats sounded. With his hand on the hilt of his sword, he turned to look behind him. White hair whipped about a woman's head as she raced to catch up with him.

When she was beside him, matching his speed, he shouted, "Who are you and why are you here?"

"We haven't been formally introduced, but I am your..." She paused as though searching for the correct words. She finally shrugged and shouted back, "I am your relative. Alastair, Tormod, and I came to help you and the Nicolsons fight the English."

"Alastair and Tormod are here?" Orrick demanded in a loud voice so she could hear him over the horses' hoofbeats. "How could they know?"

"I told them," the woman said, skilfully navigating the

patch of rocky ground they came upon in that moment. "I have been following Isolde for the past few weeks."

Orrick frowned. "Why?"

The woman's brows knit as though searching for something she'd never considered before. "As a bow-woman myself, Isolde intrigued me. As an outcast from her people, I felt sympathy for her, knowing myself what that feels like. I want to help you, if you'll allow it."

"Aren't you needed back at the battle?" Orrick kept his gaze fixed on the land before him.

"Alastair, Tormod, Graeme, and Isolde's brother have things well in hand. You, on the other hand, might have need of me."

"Then, I thank you in advance for your assistance," Orrick said with a hitch in his throat.

"You care for Isolde."

"Aye. She helped me rediscover who I am." Yet it was more than that. She'd taught him to trust himself and his abilities again. Her presence repaired a heart that first his father, and then warring had damaged. She challenged him to be a better brother, warrior, and man than he had been before. "I can't stand by and let something happen to her, not even if I have to fight the entire English army to get her back."

The woman smiled. "Then it is good you are not alone. I am Aria MacLeod."

"I might have guessed you were a MacLeod. I can see

similarities in the lines of your face." He gave a nod of his head in greeting. "I wish we had met under better circumstances so that I might get to know more about you."

"There will be time for that later. For now, we must focus on Isolde."

Orrick felt some of his tension ease. "Thank you for your help, Aria."

"While wandering the wilderness since my arrival, I discovered a faster way to the cliffs where I suspect Lieutenant Collins is taking Isolde. It is shorter, but far more treacherous."

"Show me." Orrick didn't care about the additional risk. If it closed the distance between himself and Isolde, it was an advantage he couldn't pass up.

ISOLDE WAS COLD and terrified as she and Lieutenant Collins rode past the rock formation, and the jagged coastline came back into view. He headed straight towards the cliff's edge, then brought his horse to a stop. "If anyone dared to follow you from camp, not only will they arrive too late, they will never see us behind these rocks." He dismounted and pulled Isolde to the ground. "Get up and come with me."

"Nay," she forced out past her gag. She had no reason to cooperate. She'd make killing her as difficult as she possibly could with her hands tightly bound before her.

Wind billowed up from the Sound of Raasay to buffet Isolde's hair about her face. She wished she could pull it back to see the lieutenant better, but she could imagine the look of displeasure on his face. She lifted her chin, refusing to let him see how frightened she was in this moment.

"You'll do what you're told." He drew her forward with a painful grip on her arm, towards the edge of the cliff.

Isolde dug her heels into the rocky ground, fighting him. The injury she'd delivered to his thigh made him wince as he struggled to pull harder. Which gave Isolde an idea. She went limp instead, sending the lieutenant stumbling. When he came back to her, prepared to drag her again, she kicked out, striking his injury.

He howled in pain as he clutched his thigh.

Isolde was instantly on her feet, running. There was nowhere to hide, and she wouldn't make it far before he recovered and came after her on his horse, but she would delay his plans, and hope for a miracle.

Unless he decided to simply strike her down where she stood, instead of along the dramatic cliffside. Her heart in her throat, she ran as fast as she could while working the tight ropes that bound her wrists.

Her breath came in bursts, as she struggled to pull air into her lungs around the filthy rag in her mouth. Behind her she heard hoofbeats a heartbeat before the lieutenant's hand reached down and jerked her off her feet by the hair, propelling her forward.

"I should kill you right now for that stunt, except that I want to throw your headless body over the cliff to be discovered by Orrick MacLeod." A smirk came to his lips. "That will destroy him, and in turn the MacLeods."

The lieutenant turned his horse, dragging her by her hair, and returned to the cliffs. He released her and dismounted before she could scramble to her feet. He drew his sword and instead of swinging the blade against her neck, he struck her with the hilt, forcing her back to the ground. She drew in several short, sharp breaths, trying to force the dizziness and nausea that swamped her away.

Lieutenant Collins grabbed another length of rope from his saddlebag and, taking her feet in his hands, bound them together. She kicked and writhed, but in the end, his strength overpowered her as she struggled to stay conscious.

When he was done, he sliced the gag covering her mouth, nicking her cheek. Even as she filled her lungs with fresh sea air, warm blood trickled down her cheek and neck. "When you first joined our little company as a spy, I had hoped to eventually make you mine." He ran his fingers across the cut.

She jerked her head away, trying to contain the terror that pounded in her chest. "I would rather die than let you touch me like that."

He brought the tip of his sword against her chest, pricking her once more. A blotch of red blossomed on the bodice of her gown. "You'll die, all right. As will Orrick MacLeod, and eventually all the MacLeods for refusing to acknowledge the English king. Once I report what has happened here, skewed appropriately in my favour, King George will send more regiments to not only undo the MacLeods, but all the Scots who defy him."

Isolde shook her head. "Even if you kill me, the Mac-Leods would never allow that to happen. They will do whatever it takes to stop you and your men."

"I'm counting on that." Lieutenant Collins sneered. "I'm fairly certain Orrick MacLeod will be heroic enough to follow you here and gallantly try to save you."

Fear shivered down her spine. If Orrick could, she knew he would follow her here, whether he was ready to face his demons or not. In order to defeat the lieutenant, he'd have to once again be the warrior he was before he left for the West Indies. She knew he could be, but would he have that realisation for himself?

Would it be better for her to take matters into her own hands and end this now before the lieutenant could harm the man she loved?

Her heart stumbled at the thought. A momentary smile came to her lips. The last few days with Orrick had been a gift she'd never thought she would have or even deserved. She'd learned that she was loveable and capable, no matter what her brother and the other warriors had told her all her life, and that happiness could exist for her—however short-lived. Joining her body with Orrick's had opened her to sensations beyond her wildest imagination.

In those quiet, precious moments, a part of her soul had merged with his, making him an inextricable part of herself. For that, she would be forever grateful even unto death. Meanwhile, she'd hold that feeling in her heart as she forced her panicked wits to steady and do what she had to do.

There was one last move she could carry out to guarantee Orrick remained safe, but it would come at the expense of her own life. She did not want to die—not when most everything in her life had turned in her favour. With no other options, Isolde lunged forward, hitting the lieutenant in the legs, knocking him off balance.

His face empurpled, then contorted in a snarl as she rolled across the ground and he fell backwards, towards the cliff's edge.

CHAPTER NINETEEN

T HE TRAIL ARIA had suggested they take with their
horses was nothing more than a razor's edge along the
red sandstone cliff. Below them the earth fell away at a sharp
angle that dropped onto jagged rocks far below. Orrick had
never feared heights, but a less desperate man might have
sanely turned back to more steady ground.

Neither he nor Aria talked as they concentrated on the
path before them, no wider than three of his feet placed end
to end. Phoenix stepped with caution, putting one foot in
front of the other as he skirted the edge of the abyss.

Hazy clouds scudded across the sky, and a dozen gulls
circled overhead, either awaiting a misstep that could provide
dinner for the evening, or out of sheer curiosity. Orrick
preferred to think it was the latter.

The wind added another dangerous element, forcing
Aria, Orrick, and their horses to lower their heads to protect
their eyes from bits of dirt and grit. Orrick's heart raced at
the thought of what Lieutenant Collins might be doing to
Isolde. He forced the macabre thought away to focus on a
more favourable outcome. He would find her alive and well.

They would marry as soon as he could find a minister or they would handfast. Orrick didn't want another day to pass before making Isolde his wife.

Step by step they started to ascend towards the top of the cliff along the trail. Orrick breathed a genuine sigh of relief until he raised his gaze and saw Isolde rolling towards the edge of the cliff just beyond where he and Aria rode.

"Nay!" Orrick's heart clogged his throat.

Orrick took in the scene in a single glance. He saw Lieutenant Collins toppling backwards with a crazed look in his eyes, saw Isolde rolling towards the cliff's edge.

His gaze found Isolde's and fixed on her. He would have closed his eyes and said a silent prayer that she was still alive, but that wouldn't be for long if he didn't do something, and fast.

Orrick put his heels to the horse's flanks just as Aria before him did, and they surged forward. If they could only crest the cliff at the precise moment and block their joint fall. They would save the lieutenant, but also Isolde. If they could reach them in time.

He and Aria were so close, and yet a gap still separated them.

Lieutenant Collins's body tipped over the edge, falling. He howled. The sound was a cry, high and keening—a mixture of rage, fury, and frustration.

Orrick's breath stopped as Isolde's gaze connected with his. Her eyes filled with an unfettered emotion he had never witnessed in the blue depths before . . . love.

With nothing to stop her, she fell over the edge.

Ahead of him, Aria rose up on the back of her horse, strung her bow and fired one, two, three arrows in rapid succession. The arrows hit the hem of Isolde's gown, pinning her to the edge of the sandstone cliff. Her body jerked, then hit the cliff's edge with painful force just as they reached the top.

Orrick was off his horse and diving for the edge on his knees as the sound of ripping fabric rent the air. Isolde's hands were bound. He grabbed only air until finally he seized her wrists. He held on with both hands as her falling weight yanked him closer to the edge. Orrick went down on his chest and his hands locked around hers in a vice-like grip.

The muscles of his arms screamed. Pain shot through his shoulders, but Orrick held tight. Isolde was alive, and he intended to keep her that way.

Behind him, Aria reached down and gripped Orrick's wrists, pulling both him and Isolde up as he did the same.

When they were all on the rocky ground above the cliff, Aria let go, but Orrick held tight as dizzying relief poured through him. Aria slashed the ropes at Isolde's feet, then hands. Isolde slipped her arms around him, clinging fiercely as she shivered uncontrollably.

As the sound of the waves hitting the rocks below filled the air, Orrick held tightly until Isolde's shivers died and she relaxed in his arms. Slowly, Orrick stepped back and looked down at her pale face. "Come with me."

"Where?" She gazed at him numbly for a moment.

"There is something you need to see to put all this behind you."

Isolde nodded and walked to the edge of the cliff and peered over the edge. Lieutenant Collins lay still and silent on the rocky shore some forty feet below.

"Is he dead?" she asked over the pulsing of the waves.

"That fall would kill any man."

She squeezed her eyes shut. "He's not a man. He's a monster."

"Even monsters die when they fall that far. He's gone. Soon the sea will carry his body away."

Isolde opened her eyes and gave him a half-smile before turning towards Aria. "I recognise you from the tower when the English attacked Dunvegan."

Aria nodded. "I was watching you then, as I had many times over the past few weeks."

Isolde drew a sharp breath. "I knew someone was watching me. Why would you do that? Who are you?"

Orrick eased the two of them away from the cliff and towards his relative. "Allow me to introduce you to Aria MacLeod."

"MacLeod?" Isolde frowned. "You have a female relative who is an archer and you never mentioned it?"

"I did not know about her until a short while ago. Had I known, I would have told you." Orrick smiled. "Let's return to the English encampment. By now John, Graeme, Alastair, and Tormod must have drawn that battle to a close as we have here."

Isolde raised a brow. "My brother came to help fight the English?"

Orrick nodded. "There are many things we both need additional details about, such as Aria's mysterious appearance and your brother's change of heart. Though let us hear the full story amongst the safety of our clans. Agreed?"

Isolde's lips curved. "Agreed. Before we go, I need to thank you, Aria, for saving my life. Without your arrows, I would have joined Lieutenant Collins on the rocks below."

Aria's gaze passed between Isolde and Orrick. "It was a team effort. I stopped you from falling momentarily, but Orrick halted the plummet to your death."

"I am forever beholden to you both, to be alive at this moment. I was so certain—" Isolde's voice cracked and tears sprang to her eyes.

"I'm going to gather the lieutenant's horse." Aria stepped back before turning away, giving Isolde and him some privacy.

"You came for me," Isolde said, her voice stronger now.

"I would have fought dragons for you."

She wiped away her tears. "Does this mean . . ."

"I fought my way out of Scorrybreac and through the English encampment to find you, and I will fight every day moving forward if that's what I have to do to keep you safe."

He clasped her hands in his. "You once said that I would be able to fight again if the cause was just."

She nodded.

"I would like to add that I can also fight if it means protecting my family from harm." He pulled her into an embrace. For a moment, they simply stood, wrapped in each other's arms. Orrick buried his face in her hair, breathed in her scent—blackcurrants and roses—before he slowly eased back.

"I wish I could hold you in my arms all day, but we must return and sort through the aftermath of our battle with the English. There could be grave consequences for the Scots, especially now that Lieutenant Collins is dead."

"Whatever happens, we can face it together." Isolde accepted his hand, allowing him to lead her to where Aria was already mounted and waiting. At his horse, Orrick unfastened the bow he had brought from Scorrybreac and the quiver he had retrieved from Lieutenant Collins's tent and gave them to her. "These belong with you."

"Thank you. I had given up hope of ever seeing my bow again." Her smile warmed him clear to his toes.

Orrick helped Isolde onto Phoenix's back before he swung up onto the Englishman's horse. One crisis had been avoided. What other challenges they would face before the day was through would be revealed to them all very soon. Of that, Orrick was certain.

CHAPTER TWENTY

A SHIMMER OF sunshine broke through the clouds above Isolde, Orrick, and Aria as they rode back to the English encampment. Isolde drew in an easy breath, consoled by the sound of the sea crashing against the rocks below the cliffs and the wind as it whispered across the land before them. They were comforting sounds—heralding the return to normalcy even though she doubted things in her life would ever be ordinary again. After having absolutely nothing, she would never take for granted the clothes on her back, the food at the table, or the company she kept. They were all priceless treasures she would now enjoy because of Orrick MacLeod.

As the miles passed, Isolde reflected on the past ten days since Orrick had found her in the wilderness. So much had changed in her life and in herself during that time. She was no longer isolated and alone. The wound in her arm had improved greatly. And she'd proven to herself she still retained her skill with a bow. Her wants and desires had changed as well. At one time, all she had wanted was to battle. But she'd learned that it was the calm moments—the times between the battles—that truly made life worth living.

She wanted to be a sister to her brother and an aunt to his family again, if they would allow it. More importantly, she wanted to be a wife, a lover, a friend to her future husband. To fill their lives with joy and children and adventure that had nothing to do with fighting. Yet, she also understood that battling had its place, especially in these uncertain times. Everyone—male or female—should know ways to defend not only themselves, but also those they loved, should the need ever arise.

With a renewed sense of purpose, Isolde, Orrick, and Aria approached the English encampment. The site was strangely quiet as they approached. Orrick must have sensed something was off as well because he drew his sword. Isolde and Aria both strung their bows. It wasn't until they passed several tents that they finally saw Alastair and Tormod near a cluster of English soldiers guarded by Graeme and the MacLeod warriors. The Englishmen were bound at the wrists and tied in pairs as they sat upon the ground.

At the sight of the riders, all eyes turned their direction. Alastair separated himself from the men and came towards them. "I see you were successful in your rescue of Isolde," Alastair said, greeting her with a welcoming smile. "We are all very relieved to see you safe, my lady." He paused, then asked, "Where is Lieutenant Collins?"

"He's dead. He fell over a cliff and to his death," Isolde said from atop Orrick's horse.

"What happened here?" Orrick asked, sliding down from the Englishman's horse before helping Isolde down. She was grateful for the assistance, since all the fight earlier had left her suddenly drained of her strength. As though sensing her need for a moment of stability before he let go, Orrick's arm slipped about her waist.

Alastair's features sobered. "The English are defeated. Only three and twenty of the original company of men remain alive. John and the Nicolson warriors are gathering the dead. We must see them to their final reward before we head back to Dunvegan with our prisoners."

"We cannot free the Englishmen, can we?" Orrick asked.

Alastair shook his head. "If we release them, they would only return to England and bring back many more troops that we Scots are not ready to confront. We need time to gather weapons and prepare for an all-out war with England. These men will not be missed in their homeland for a while. That affords us time we desperately need."

"Where will you put the prisoners? Dunvegan is growing crowded after taking in so many villagers who have fallen victim to clan attacks as of late."

Alastair's gaze passed between Isolde and Orrick. "Am I correct in assuming there is something developing between you two? The kiss I witnessed the other day suggested that you clearly care for each other."

Isolde felt her cheeks heat at the memory of that fiery kiss.

Orrick pulled her closer against his side and smiled, warming all the parts of her that had chilled on their ride back to the encampment. "Isolde has agreed to be my wife."

Alastair returned his brother's smile. "Many felicitations. Gwendolyn will be pleased to hear that news. When will you wed?"

"Tonight. As soon as we return to Dunvegan," Orrick said, his eyes glowing with eagerness.

Instead of objecting, Alastair's smile grew. "I remember my own haste to marry Gwendolyn. I didn't want to chance something stopping us for a second time." He nodded. "There will be a wedding at Dunvegan tonight."

Alastair's face became serious once more. "As for where to put the prisoners. I was hoping to discuss this with you at a less urgent time . . . I do have a solution to our overcrowding problem at Dunvegan."

Orrick's brow rose with interest. "What is that?"

"Geordie, our solicitor, has been combing through the estate's papers that were in disorder after Father died. In doing so, he has uncovered several properties Father must have purchased in secret or won through conflicts with other clans. One of those castles is a fortress to the north-west of Dunvegan, near Halistra. I would like you and Isolde to go there with the prisoners and start your new life there." His voice was suddenly urgent. "You were right to say that Tormod and I always forced you into the shadows. Looking back now, we both see that we made it impossible for you to be your own man."

Orrick tensed beside her. "You are giving me a castle of my own and the responsibility of overseeing our enemy?"

Alastair nodded. "The castle and a settlement from Father's estate. You deserve that and so much more."

Orrick shook his head dazedly. "Isolde and I will gladly take the prisoners there."

"Not alone. I am sending an additional fifty seasoned warriors, several young men who need training, and many of the villagers we are harbouring at Dunvegan who wish to better their lives while being protected by not one, but two great warriors."

"I would go with you, if you would have me," Aria said, joining them.

Alastair turned to Aria. "I had selfishly hoped you would remain at Dunvegan so that we might get to know you, and you your human family. However, if you would rather go with Orrick and Isolde. It sounds like you have been a prisoner to others' desires for far too long. I will not stand in the way of your wishes."

Aria's eyes widened, filled with disbelief and then pleasure. "Then I will remain at Dunvegan, with the majority of my clan." She turned to Orrick. "However, if you ever have need of me, I will come at any time to aid you."

Isolde watched as the remaining shadows in Orrick's eyes cleared. The pain he'd carried with him that had nothing to do with the West Indies vanished. She suddenly realised how desperate Orrick had been to be an equal with his brothers. She knew that feeling well enough. Orrick and the Mac-Leods had given her everything she'd ever wanted, and now Orrick would have his dreams come true also.

Orrick turned to Isolde, his gaze searching her face. "Do you agree to this plan? Whatever we do, we will do it together."

"All I have ever wanted was to use my skills and abilities as a warrior to help Scotland and her people. So, aye. This is a duty and an honour we can both share."

Orrick kissed her, a brief salute that hinted at more to come later. "We accept." With a more serious look, he stepped away from Isolde and shifted his gaze to Alastair. "For any of this to happen, we must first bury the dead and take down any evidence of this encampment."

Alastair nodded. "Would you and Isolde help the men in taking down the tents while Aria and I help the men bury the dead?"

"Before I help with the encampment, might I go to my brother? We have a few things that need to be said between us. We've waited too long already."

"Of course," Alastair said with a look of understanding. He pointed off to the left, behind a row of tents that had yet to be taken down. "John is over there with his men, digging graves."

It didn't take Isolde long to spot a familiar head of brown hair threaded with grey amongst the men digging near the trees.

When John saw her, he stopped and threw his shovel aside, rushing to greet her. "Isolde. You have no idea how glad I am to see you alive." Her brother pulled her into his arms in the first embrace he had ever given her. She was so startled that it took a moment before she returned his show of affection.

"I am glad to see you are unharmed also." Isolde drew a slow, even breath in an effort to regain her composure before she pulled back and studied her brother. Concern and weariness were written into the very texture of his face.

"Why did you come after me, John? I thought you were the one who set the trap so that Lieutenant Collins could abduct me."

"He forced me to take you to the chapel. He said he only wanted to talk to you, but I should have known better. The man was frothing with plans for vengeance." John looked away. "I guess I was looking for a way to get back at you after all that we've been through at the castle for the past year."

Isolde frowned. "Why didn't you and your men fight him?"

"Because we lost the best warrior we had, and the soul of our defence, when I forced you to leave. No one wanted to take on the English, so we chose to suffer instead."

John sighed. "That was the first moment I realised not only what I had done to you, but also the ramifications of my actions on everyone at Scorrybreac. I was jealous of your abilities. And I just wanted to be rid of you. Marriage to Ewen MacPhee seemed the easiest way to make that happen." John shook his head wearily. "If you had been with us, you would have fought your way out, no matter the obstacle. We did look for you. When the hunting parties went out, they tried to locate you, but you were nowhere to be found."

John frowned. "Only yesterday Lieutenant Collins revealed that he had captured you when you left and that he'd forced you to become a spy against your own people for him."

"I escaped."

John's lips pulled up in a momentary smile. "Of course you did. You would never willingly work with the English to bring harm to this country or her people."

"I stayed with the English at first, because they threatened to label you as a traitor if I didn't. But after my reports sent the chief of Clan MacTavish to gaol, and after I misinterpreted the English outside Scorrybreac to mean that you had sided with Lieutenant Collins, I went where no one would find me."

"You had to escape. I understand that," John said gravely. "When we failed to find you, that was the second time I realised none of this would have come to pass if I had only held on to my temper. I was just so angry."

"You thought my negligence hurt you, your wife, and your child."

John shook his head. "Then the moment you returned to

us, you saw something was wrong with Brea that none of us could resolve. You healed her. You saved her leg, and quite possibly her life. That was the third time I chastised myself for my foolishness. Had you been with us, you might have spared Brea from the pain she's had to endure her whole life."

A wave of sorrow moved though Isolde. "I am sorry I hurt Brea. Ewen ruined my aim in an effort to cheat in the contest you'd set up for the two of us."

John looked away. "The moment before your arrows came at me and Sarah, I thought I saw Ewen move closer to you, but I refused to believe my own eyes. Now I wish I had."

"Nevertheless, my arrows caused you all much pain."

Her brother's eyes glittered with tears. "I caused you pain as well by banishing you. Will you ever forgive me?"

Isolde took her brother's hands in hers and held them tight. She held his gaze, hoping he could see there was no blame in her expression, only forgiveness. "John, if it wasn't for you, and all of what happened to us, I would never have become the warrior I am today. Living alone in the wilderness honed my skills. It also brought me Orrick MacLeod. If you agree to come to Dunvegan, I ask that you give me away at my wedding to Orrick tonight."

"It would be my privilege to walk you down the aisle, and aye. I most heartily agree to this arrangement."

She laughed, feeling a deep sense of rightness. "I want to

be involved in your and Sarah's lives from now on. And, if you will allow it, I would love to train my niece how to use a weapon to defend herself."

John joined in her laughter. "As your brother, I did not see the advantages of such a thing for a female. Now, as a parent, I long for my child to know how to keep herself safe. So, aye, I whole-heartedly support you training her when she is old enough."

A smile still on his lips, he embraced her once more, then released her. "We had best finish our tasks here because we have a wedding to attend by nightfall."

Isolde drew a breath and let joy flood her spirit. A wedding. Her wedding. But it was more than that. She was no longer alone in this life, she was surrounded by family, both Nicolsons and MacLeods, and she was accepted for who she was—a female warrior who would protect her family and the people of Scotland in the years ahead.

Who could ask for anything more?

<hr />

ARIA STOOD BESIDE Alastair, Tormod, and Orrick. Her family. People who accepted her for who she was at the moment. Would they still feel the same when she told them about their brother? After all, she was also a part of the fairy world who had taken the babe from them.

Clutching her hands before her, Aria cleared her throat.

"Before another moment passes, there is something I need to tell you all."

Alastair drew closer. "We are listening."

"When I first came to this realm, my heart was filled with vengeance. I wanted revenge against your father for not taking me in years ago."

"That is only natural," Tormod said. "Our father was unfair to you. Our mother told us of how you suffered in the fairy world because of your heritage."

"I am not the only one who suffers," Aria said.

Orrick frowned as he studied her face. "What do you mean?"

Aria drew a steadying breath as she fisted her hands, hoping they would not hate her for her next words. "Your brother, Keiran is alive and living in Fairyland."

"Keiran's alive?" they all echoed in unison.

"Is he all right?" Alastair asked, concern etched into the lines of his face.

Aria nodded. "He was stolen from his crib in retribution by the fairy king when he discovered my mother had brought me to the human realm and intended to leave me there. He has been raised by the king as his own son." She omitted the part of the story where Keiran had been designated as her bridegroom.

"Does Mother know this?" Orrick asked.

Again Aria nodded. "I told her when I entered Dunvegan Castle. I was waiting to tell the rest of you when the time was right." She offered them a half-smile. "Now is not the perfect time, but I could wait no longer."

"Thank you for telling us now." Alastair looked at each of his brothers. "Is it possible to retrieve him from Fairyland?"

Aria straightened. "With the help of a fairy."

"Then let us go retrieve him right now," Tormod said.

"Is Keiran safe for the moment?" Alastair asked.

"I doubt the king would ever harm his own adopted son, but he has had to endure the same sort of abuse as I have from the other fairies. But being fully human, I can only imagine their taunts were even worse than those I suffered."

"I'll round up some men. We should go to Fairyland tonight." A flare of anger passed through Tormod's eyes.

"Nay." Alastair stayed his brother with a hand. "Tonight is for Orrick and Isolde. I am fairly convinced that Keiran is safe enough where he is. Let us come up with a well-thought-out plan, with Aria's help, to enter Fairyland and successfully retrieve our brother. Agreed?" Alastair looked at his brothers, waiting for their agreement.

When Orrick and Tormod both nodded, Alastair turned back to Aria. "Thank you for telling us about our brother. We are so grateful that you not only helped us this day, but that you will also help us in the future."

The tension that had filled Aria earlier slipped away. "It is what family does—they help each other in times of need."

"Do Rowena or Callum know about Keiran?" Tormod

asked.

"Nay."

A smile pulled up the corners of Tormod's mouth and brought a spark of mischief to his eyes. "I cannot wait to tell them not only about Keiran, but also that Rowena finally has that sister she has forever been longing for."

"And that Callum will no longer be the baby of the family."

Aria bit down on her lip. Should she also tell them that Keiran had been magically aged to be their own equal? The human side of her wanted to force the words out, but the fairy side of her, the mischievous side, won out and kept her silent. The MacLeod triplets would discover that fact in time.

"Come, brothers, we have a wedding to prepare for," Alastair said with a note of cheer that had been missing from his voice before she'd told him about his brother. At least some good had come from today. Isolde was alive. She and Orrick would marry tonight. Aria had been accepted into the MacLeod clan fold. And the English would be subdued for a time.

They had much to celebrate even though danger still lurked in the shadows for the MacLeod clan.

CHAPTER TWENTY-ONE

N IGHT HAD FALLEN and a million stars filled the sky as the MacLeods and the Nicolsons finished the burials and taking down the encampment. There was no longer a trace that the English had ever been there. The mood in the air was sombre. They'd spent themselves physically by not only battling but by the work afterwards. Orrick was thankful for all those who had come to support both him and Isolde. Without them, the day's outcome might have been very different.

As they headed back to Dunvegan, Orrick scanned the faces of those who rode with Isolde and him. These men and the two women looked exhausted and wanted nothing more than a warm hearth, a hearty meal, a mug of ale, and a good night's sleep as their reward. Yet as they approached the castle, their tired mumbles became excited chatter at the sight that greeted them there.

Gwendolyn, Fiona, and Rowena waited outside, dressed in brightly coloured gowns. The approach to the castle was lit with torches. They greeted everyone as the travellers entered the courtyard and directed them towards several large tubs of warmed water that had been set out for their cleansing.

Before Orrick could dismount, Rowena helped Isolde down and whisked her away inside the castle. Though a sense of disappointment rippled through him, Orrick had to admit once he'd taken his turn at the washing stations, that the water combined with the cool night air renewed his spirit.

When they were finished, the men were invited into the great hall where they were greeted by Mrs Honey and her staff for a feast of boar's head, minced pies, salmon, herring, rabbit stew, roasted onions, bread and cheese, and ale, and frumenty for dessert. Tallow candles set in pairs about the chamber gave the great hall a warm and magical air.

It was made all the more magical when the once-exhausted men entered the chamber, greeting the others with good cheer and laughter. Callum and Rowena were there, sitting alongside their mother, who hovered more than sat at the table. Gwendolyn's siblings, Arabella and Samuel, were there also seated nearby. Graeme and Geordie were deep in conversation at the far end of the table. And Mrs Morgan, Becks, and Lottie joined them as well instead of eating belowstairs with the staff. John Nicolson joined Callum, Alastair, and Tormod while the Nicolson warriors and the MacLeod warriors filled the long tables all around the hall. Orrick looked out at the sea of green and blue and red and green—the MacLeods and the Nicolson clans were no longer allies, but kin.

A warm smile came to Orrick's lips. He'd had many feasts in this great hall, but none had ever filled him with such hope and excitement as this one did. Tonight he and Isolde would join their lives forever. Dunvegan had seen many difficult times in the past few months, but as of late, it had also been filled with joy and celebration that had helped push those bad times into the distant past.

From across the chamber, Isolde entered the room with Gwendolyn on one side and Fiona on the other. She had washed and was dressed in a heather-coloured gown that enhanced the fullness of her breasts, the narrowness of her waist, and clung to her well-toned hips before falling to the floor in waves of fabric. Her hair was swept up in a smooth twist at the back of her head. It was near impossible to reconcile the woman he'd met in the wilderness with the beautiful, refined, and elegant vision before him. When her gaze met his, her smile was warm, and bright.

Orrick moved across the floor to her side. With each step he took he felt himself changing, evolving. The shadows and memories of his past fell away, and light—pure and hot and white—flooded his body, illuminating places deep inside that had been cold and dark for years. For the first time in his life he knew what he wanted, and more importantly, he felt as though he deserved it.

When he reached her, he took her hands in his, and the rest of the room seemed to fade away, until there was only the two of them. "Isolde."

"I am so pleased to finally have time to talk to you in relative privacy. There are so many things I long to say."

"Me as well."

She took his hands in hers. "I cannot quite believe that I am still alive to say this . . . Before I fell over the edge of the cliff, I realised I never said the words. I love you, Orrick MacLeod. With all my heart."

Orrick pulled her into his arms. He tilted his head so that his gaze lingered on his bride-to-be. She sparkled with joy, and the sight made his chest unaccountably tight. "And I love you, my brave warrior." He touched his lips to hers. *His beloved. His heart.*

As soon as supper was through, Rowena led those gathered out to the rear courtyard. She draped a warm cloak about Isolde's shoulders and held her back with Orrick while the others passed through the rear door to the outside.

Clusters of candles had been set along the edge of the rear courtyard and the wall, bathing the area in a golden glow. With the stars overhead against a veil of black and the candles all around, the scene was more than breathtaking, it was magical.

Much to Orrick's surprise, Reverend Vollar stood, waiting, near the crenellated wall. Orrick turned to Rowena. "How did you know that we wanted to marry tonight?"

Rowena smiled. "You are not as mysterious as you'd like to think, Brother." She waved him outside while continuing to hold Isolde back.

Once Orrick stepped outside, Rowena offered Isolde a small bouquet of Lenten roses that were a light rose purple mixed with leathery evergreen foliage. "Winter roses?"

"They are not truly roses, yet they reminded Gwendolyn, Fiona, and me of you—a flower so strong it blooms in the winter." Rowena smiled. "Are you ready to get married?"

Isolde's heart caught. She'd never been more ready for anything in her life. She stepped outside and was greeted by her brother.

"I never thought I'd see this day," John said with a smile.

Isolde never imagined she would see her brother smile like that again—at least not at her. "My only regret is that Mother and Father are not here."

"They are here with us. I know they are. And they are so proud of the woman you've become." John took her arm and held her steady as she made her way to Orrick.

The rest of the ceremony passed quickly. Bathed in light, she and Orrick stood together as the minister gave them his blessing. Wrapped in the glow of Orrick's love, Isolde allowed him to slide a gold band on her finger. "This was my mother's ring. She wants you to have it." When he was done, he brought her hand to his lips and placed a kiss atop the ring he had just given her. "I will try to be worthy of your love for the rest of my days."

She sought out Orrick's mother, who hovered near the front of those gathered. Isolde nodded her thanks, but just as she was about to look away, the woman's translucent skin shifted from grey to a softer cream, almost as if the woman once again had flesh.

She wasn't the only one who noticed as several gasps issued from those gathered. "Mother?" Orrick asked. "What is happening to you?"

I do not know. She stared down at her hands, turning them over and back again.

Callum came forward, trying to lift one of those hands. It was still vaporous even though it looked more solid than it ever had before. "Haven't you noticed?" Callum said, looking at his siblings. "Every time one of her children finds contentment, our mother grows more and more humanlike?"

Alastair's brows came together. "Is that why you are here? To see us all settled and happy?"

I do not know why I remain with all of you, but we are not here to talk about me. We are here to join Orrick and Isolde as husband and wife.

Silence settled over those gathered and all eyes shifted back to Isolde and Orrick. As Reverend Vollar pronounced them husband and wife, Orrick held nothing back. He kissed her firmly, telling her more clearly than words how fervently he loved her. Isolde kissed him back, and when finally he broke the kiss, she whispered against his lips, "Do not think that now that we are man and wife I will let you win any future battles just to spare your manly pride."

"I have already won the only battle I ever wanted to, and that was convincing you to be my wife."

Isolde grinned at him. "There will be other battles."

He laughed out loud, holding her close. "I'm counting on it."

Wrapped in Orrick's love, she looked up at the night sky, feeling as if the moon and the stars overhead twinkled just for the two of them and the bright future they would share.

EPILOGUE

Four months later

BEHIND THE THICK grey stone walls of Dunshee Castle near the village of Halistra, Isolde MacLeod stood in the large training area that she and Orrick had built since they'd come to their new home. Her students stood on one side of the open area while Orrick's stood on the other.

Isolde looked out over her students and smiled. Since news had leaked out amongst the clans of a female warrior who had defeated the English, women of all ages had come to Dunshee, seeking her out, asking her to train them in the ways of battle.

It was a dream come true. No longer was she an oddity amongst her people, she was someone her people looked up to and tried to emulate. Amongst her students today were Emlyn and Brea.

"I cannot believe how much stronger Brea has become since she's been training with you," her sister-in-law Sarah said from beside Isolde.

"It is a miracle, isn't it?" Isolde's chest tightened with pride at the sight of the eighteen-month-old as she toddled at the edge of the training arena with her wooden sword, trying to best a very tolerant Emlyn. Brea's leg bore a scar, but there were no lasting effects from the putrid wound that had poisoned her body for so long.

Having finished her lessons for the day, Emlyn now played with Brea, teaching her simple manoeuvres that often dissolved into bouts of laughter. Even though she now played, Emlyn was well on her way to becoming a gifted swordswoman. She took instruction well and practised hard, and had already won battles against women three times her age.

"What you are doing here with these women is the miracle." Sarah's voice filled with awe. "We might actually have a chance of defeating the English thanks to what you and Orrick have started here."

While Isolde trained the women, Orrick trained the men. He'd started with the warriors Alastair had sent along with them to Dunshee Castle. But just as the women came to her, the country's men came to him. "We are simply doing our part to help make sure Scotland remains free now and in the future."

"How are the English settling into their life as prisoners here?" Sarah asked, her expression suddenly serious.

"They are treated well. They are not forced to live in a dark prison, but locked inside one of the barracks. They have beds to sleep on with plenty of blankets. Orrick has shared his very large collection of books with them. We feed them well and allow them to exercise once a day."

"You and Orrick are generous. I've heard awful tales of how the English treat the Scots whom they capture."

Isolde raised her chin. "That is not how we wish to be remembered. The Englishmen know they are fortunate, and have thanked us occasionally for treating them with respect. But they also know they won't be here forever. War is coming and there is nothing any of us can do to stop it."

"A war of the clans or a war with England?" Sarah asked.

"It could be both." Isolde tightened her lips. "For now though, we are at peace. Let us live each and every day to the fullest and not borrow trouble from the future."

"I couldn't agree with you more, my heart," Orrick said, coming up behind her and wrapping his arms around her waist. "The future is yet unwritten. For now, I'd like to keep it that way."

Again, they were in total agreement. What they had now was special. Precious. Nothing and no one could take that away from them.

THE END

Want more? Check out Alastair and Gwendolyn's story in *The Return of the Heir*!

Join Tule Publishing's newsletter for more great reads and weekly deals!

AUTHOR'S NOTE

Dunvegan Castle on the Isle of Skye has been home to the MacLeod clan for the last eight hundred years. Throughout those turbulent centuries, the fortress has guarded the clan's most precious treasure. The Fairy Flag of Dunvegan might look like a faded, battered bit of cloth with a few strange markings, but it holds a mystery that has turned into a legend.

The legend the MacLeods believe is true is that the cloth was given to them by a fairy princess after she was forced to leave her child with Iain Cair MacLeod in the human realm. The flag is said to possess magic that can help the clan when it is waved three times by a flagbearer at a time of great need.

The Fairy Flag has been used twice before and it is said that the fragile flag on display at Dunvegan Castle has but a single miracle left to give.

If you enjoyed *To Win a Highlander's Heart*,
you'll love the next book in the...

GUARDIANS OF THE ISLES SERIES

Book 1: *The Return of the Heir*

Book 2: *Only a Highlander Will Do*

Book 3: *To Win a Highlander's Heart*

Book 4: *To Claim His Highland Bride*
Coming in February 2023!

Available now at your favorite online retailer!

MORE BOOKS BY GERRI RUSSELL

ALL THE KINGS MEN SERIES
Book 1: *Seven Nights with a Scot*

Book 2: *Romancing the Laird*

Book 3: *A Temptress in Tartan*

Book 4: *A Laird and a Gentleman*

Book 5: *Much Ado About a Scot*

Available now at your favorite online retailer!

ABOUT THE AUTHOR

Barbara Roser Photography

Gerri Russell is the award-winning author of historical and contemporary novels including the Brotherhood of the Scottish Templars series and *Flirting with Felicity*. A two-time recipient of the Romance Writers of America's Golden Heart Award and winner of the American Title II competition sponsored by *RT Book Reviews* magazine, she is best known for her adventurous and emotionally intense novels set in the thirteenth- and fourteenth-century Scottish Highlands. Before Gerri followed her passion for writing romance novels, she worked as a broadcast journalist, a newspaper reporter, a magazine columnist, a technical writer and editor, and an instructional designer. She lives in the Pacific Northwest with her husband and four mischievous black cats.

Thank you for reading

TO WIN A HIGHLANDER'S HEART

If you enjoyed this book, you can find more from all our great authors at TulePublishing.com, or from your favorite online retailer.

TULE
PUBLISHING